THE MOST WONDERFUL TIME OF THE YEAR

After ditching her cheating boyfriend, Sara escapes to a small village for Christmas, expecting to find rest and relaxation without the usual seasonal stresses. But her landlady, Emma, soon involves her in the village's holiday preparations, and the magic of Christmas begins to weave its spell. While Sara settles in and makes new friends, she also relishes the special attentions of Emma's handsome neighbour, Alex, and his young daughter. Could she actually have a future here — and is this Christmas destined to be her best ever?

WENDY KREMER

THE MOST WONDERFUL TIME OF THE YEAR

Complete and Unabridged

LINFORD
Leicester

First published in Great Britain in 2015

First Linford Edition
published 2017

A catalogue record for this book is available
from the British Library.

ISBN 978–1–4448–3507–6

Published by
F. A. Thorpe (Publishing)
Anstey, Leicestershire

Set by Words & Graphics Ltd.
Anstey, Leicestershire
Printed and bound in Great Britain by
T. J. International Ltd., Padstow, Cornwall

This book is printed on acid-free paper

1

The house was unembellished grey stone. At first glance it seemed daunting, but the bright curtains and the shiny green door did much to soften the impression. Sara recalled briefly how it felt to go home to her parents' small squat cottage in the Cotswolds at Christmas. The contrast between this house and theirs couldn't be greater.

Well, this was what she wanted, wasn't it? A quiet place in a strange locality, to spend Christmas where no one knew her.

Sara got out of her warm Mini and grabbed her coat from the back seat. The strong chilly breeze blowing from the direction of the moorlands behind the house flapped it about when she buttoned it up, and she slipped her hands under the sheepskin collar to tighten it around her neck. She shivered, but started to feel more protected and warmer by the time she'd lifted her holdall out of the boot. The gate was open. She walked determinedly up the flagged pathway bordered by plants that were hibernating for the winter. Gusts of wind blew strands of her auburn hair across her face. She shoved them impatiently aside with her free hand and paused in the small protective porch that shielded the front door.

Just at that moment, a tall man came round the corner of the house and halted suddenly. He seemed a bit annoyed to find her on the doorstep, but perhaps that was just her imagination working overtime. It was more likely that he already knew there wasn't enough room for two people on the porch and he'd have to stand in the gusty wind. She noted his lean features, dark eyes and guarded expression. His thick black hair flew uncontrolled in the blustery wind, and there wasn't much welcome in his expression. If this was her host-to-be, she might end up voluntarily spending Christmas in her room, with some books and a glass of wine.

He muttered something that might have been 'Morning,' but she wasn't sure, so she just nodded and lifted the solid brass knocker. The door flew open, and a cheery middle-aged woman in unpretentious clothes, and with a neat grey hairstyle, smiled at her. 'You must be Miss Holden?'

Sara nodded. 'And you're Mrs Arber?'

'That's right. I'm Emma. Come in out of the cold!'

Sara gave her a smile. 'Gladly!' She stepped inside and was delighted to find herself enveloped in a blanket of warm air. 'It's lovely and cosy in here. I'm Sara.'

The older woman nodded. 'Dump your bag over there and come into the kitchen. I expect you'd like a cup of tea after your journey?'

'That would be wonderful.'

Emma began to close the door and then noticed there was still someone on the doorstep. Surprised, she re-opened it and said, 'Alex, what are you doing here?'

Alex had a deep voice, and Sara also discovered he had a lovely smile — even if it wasn't directed at her.

'I've come to fix the shed. I knocked on the kitchen door but there was no answer, so I thought I'd check here, before I go home again.'

Sara adjusted her initial conjecture; he was probably an odd-job man. He was too young to be Emma's husband.

Emma said, 'I haven't unlocked the back door yet. I've been upstairs, getting things ready for my visitors. You've chosen a rotten day to work outside, lad. It's so cold and windy, and there's not much chance it'll improve either.'

Sara stood listening to them and glanced briefly at the man's face with its aesthetic lines. He was younger than she first imagined — probably in his early thirties or thereabouts. It was clear they knew each other well, so if he wasn't her host, he was either a good friend who was helping her landlady, or he could be Emma's son.

He brushed Emma's protest aside. 'The weather won't improve much in the next couple of days according to the forecast. If I don't do it now, I won't have time until after Christmas. It's up to you, of course, but I'm guessing it won't take long. You mentioned that it's catching, and dragging across the slabs?'

'Yes. I didn't want to bother you, but I keep my bike in there. At present, I battle with the blasted door for ages just to put my bike away or get it out.'

He gave Emma a smile and his white teeth flashed briefly. Whatever the connection was, as well as being attractive, he was clearly kind-hearted and helpful.

'You should forget your bike in this kind of weather. Come to the supermarket with me, or go with Ken.'

'I need my bike for lots of things every day, you know that. I haven't had a cold in years. I put that down to going everywhere by bike, in all kinds of weather. I did think once about buying a car, but my bike suits me fine, keeps me fit, and it costs me nothing. If you're determined to fix it now, don't stay out there too long, Alex, or you'll catch a cold. Katie will be devastated if you end up in bed over Christmas. She's getting more excited with every passing day. Where is she, by the way?'

'I just dropped her off at the school. They're choosing who's going to play who in the nativity play. I don't envy Megan this afternoon. Katie's absolutely certain she's going to be Mary. I keep telling her she's too small and young, but she won't listen.'

Emma's face creased into a sudden smile. 'Yes, I know. She's been on about it for days. I keep telling her there are at least twenty others with the same wish, but it doesn't do much good.' Remembering her new visitor, she turned to Sara and said, 'This is Alex Crossley. He's my neighbour, and Katie is his five-year-old daughter. She started school this autumn.'

A feeling of anticlimax formed inside Sara when she heard he was married with a little girl, and she wondered why. She told Emma, 'We met outside already. Hello!'

Emma also put Alex in the picture. 'This is Sara Holden. She's staying with me over Christmas.'

He glanced at Sara and noted the friendly green eyes and thick dark lashes in an oval face with creamy skin. He nodded briefly. 'Hi!' He returned his attention to Emma. 'I've got to pick Katie up in less than an hour, so I'm not likely to die of exposure, am I? I left my toolbox out the back, and I don't think it'll take long.' Without further ado, he headed off down the passage-way.

Emma told Sara, 'Hang your coat over there and follow me.'

Sara did. She trailed after Emma down the tiled hallway into a cosy kitchen where a Rayburn produced the heat and cosiness that were heartwarming on a day like this. There was the aroma of something delicious floating in the air. It smelt like a rich casserole with lots of carrots and onions. Sara decided things were improving in leaps and bounds.

Emma gestured her towards a farmhouse chair next to the scrubbed wooden table, and bustled around making tea and arranging the tea things. 'Did you have a good journey? I hope you'll enjoy your stay and won't get bored. There isn't much organized entertainment for young people hereabouts at this time of year.'

Sara smiled. 'That's one reason why I came — for some peace and quiet. When I spotted your advert in the magazine, I knew it was just what I needed. Somewhere off the beaten track, without all the stress and commercial pressures of Christmas.'

Emma chuckled and took an immediate liking to her young visitor. She had beautiful reddish-brown hair and bright eyes. She was smart and stylish — a townie — but without the flamboyant tastes that often went with town dwellers. 'I expect you'll find it's quieter here, but we still go mad at this time of year. Christmas traditions in the countryside are firmly established. Our vicar is almost a physical wreck by the New Year. He's a widower who thinks he has to keep everyone in the parish happy. That's a juggling act, because he tries to attend all the local events leading up to Christmas, and he's often involved in organizing them too.'

Sara looked around the spotless kitchen, and her glance rested on a Welsh dresser with its display of blue and white china. It was a real eye-catcher. 'That sounds like pure stress to me, especially if he isn't particularly interested in whatever he's attending.'

'Oh, Paul is very philosophical. He

enjoys being with people, and I don't think he reflects much on what the various groups and associations do. The people are important to him, not why they come.'

'Then he's an ideal vicar, and it sounds like he's dedicated to his job. Personally, I'm glad I've escaped all the last-minute present-buying and travelling. This is the first time I've celebrated Christmas without my family.' Sara noted Emma's unspoken curiosity, so she went on to explain. 'My parents are in the Caribbean. My sister Liz and I gave them a cruise as a silver-wedding present. We deliberately chose a Christmas trip so that they could relax after all the fuss. My mother got in a real tizzy over it. Liz already had an invitation to go to her boyfriend's family over Christmas, so I made up my mind not to stand in the way. She doesn't know I've come here; otherwise I'm sure she would have changed her plans. She thinks I'll be celebrating with friends of mine. I'm free to do what I like, for the first time ever.'

Emma poured them tea. 'And you don't have a boyfriend?'

Reminded of Rod, Sara felt annoyance and resentment rising again. 'Not anymore. I found out quite recently he was double-dealing. He'd been having an affair with one of our clients and playing me along at the same time.'

Emma sat down and pushed a plate of digestive biscuits across the table. 'Well I hope you enjoy your stay with me. And you should be thankful you found out about your boyfriend, before it was too late.'

Sara reached for a biscuit, not understanding why it was so easy to talk to Emma about breaking up with Rod. Perhaps it was because she was a stranger. She hadn't yet told her parents or her sister about Rod. They'd only met him once — at the silver-wedding celebrations, and they all thought he was great. He had impressed them with his best behaviour.

Sara sipped her tea and glanced outside. A tree with bare branches alongside the window tapped on the glass and fought with the gusts of wind. She could see Alex, busy with a drill. He'd already lifted the old shed door out of its frame and positioned it against the wall. She shrugged. 'Yes, I know — you're perfectly right. I thought I'd be upset and that I'd miss him dreadfully, but I don't. I wonder now if I ever really cared for him in the right way.'

'Life doesn't always run in a straight line, does it? My husband died from a heart attack when he was just forty-six. It was an awful shock and I still miss him. You just met Alex. He was young with a successful business. He had a pretty wife, a beautiful house, a baby and no financial worries. Then the doctors found out that his wife Sue had a brain tumour. She died two months after it was diagnosed.'

Sara's eyes widened. 'Gosh! How awful!'

'Yes, we were all shocked. She was such a nice girl, and Katie was barely two when it happened. She can't remember much about her mother anymore, but Alex tries to keeps her memory alive with pictures and stories. He's a great father. Sometimes I think he's too protective, but I suppose that's understandable.'

'Hm! I had an impression that he was reserved, but if he's suffered a knock like that . . . '

'Oh, he was always serious and very dependable. He also has a great sense of humour when you know him better. We still don't see quite as much of that as we did before his wife died, but he's coming round gradually, and I'm glad to see Alex's optimism and fun emerging again these days.'

'It must be difficult for him to cope with day-to-day life on his own with a young daughter.'

'He's very organized — has to be. He owns and runs a small engineering firm. Until Katie was old enough to go to nursery school, he worked from home a lot. He juggled his time between the company and home, and could always depend on both sets of parents to babysit whenever he had appointments or meetings. Once Katie started nursery school, he asked me to pick her up and look after her until he fetched her after work. She's no trouble and she's a sweet little lass. She started school a few months ago. Now he drops her off there on his way to work. He pays me, and it suits us both fine. He knows that if something holds him up, it makes no difference to me. He can concentrate on work without worrying about Katie all the time.'

'I see.'

'He often does small repairs for me, like today. I let him, because even though he pays me for looking after Katie, I think it makes him feel better. If I had to get a professional to do all the minor jobs that he does, I'd soon be out of pocket. My son Ken is useless when it comes to mending anything; he doesn't know the difference between a chisel and a screwdriver. He's got a clever brain though, and works for a big insurance company in the next town to us. He lives there now.'

Sara drained her cup and shook her head when Emma lifted the pot for another cup. 'No, thanks. That was lovely.'

'I expect you'd like to see your room and unpack your bag?'

Sara nodded and got up.

'We have our evening meal at six. Is that all right with you? Another married couple arrived a couple of hours ago. They've gone to the village for some newspapers. I'm still waiting for a nice young man who spent his summer holiday here this year and wanted to come back for Christmas. So you won't be on your own.'

'I wouldn't mind that.' Sara looked out of the window and noticed that Alex was struggling with the door. He was trying to hold it up and fix the screws at the same time. 'It looks like he could do with an extra hand.'

Emma looked over her shoulder. 'Probably! But he'd never ask.'

'That's silly. He can't manage on his own. I'll get my coat.'

Emma nodded approvingly.

Sara buttoned herself into her coat again and tightened the collar. She thrust her hands into a pair of old woollen gloves she found in one of the pockets and hurried out into yard. Alex was muttering to himself and trying to juggle with the door and the drill at the same time. The door looked pretty solid and heavy. He looked up.

'Can I help? We saw you struggling, and I wondered if you'd like me to hold the door while you fix the screws. Or you can hold the door and I'll fix the screws, if you prefer.' The wind rocketed round the corner of the outhouse to untidy her hair and whip colour into her face.

He deliberated for a moment. 'Do you know how to use a drill?'

'Yes, I've hung pictures and assembled

bits of furniture. If you hold the door, I'll fix the first couple of screws and you can do the rest.' She stuffed her gloves back into her pocket and held out her hand for the drill.

He nodded silently. The wind blew his hair around crazily, and he watched carefully as she positioned a screw on the drill's magnetic end. Satisfied that she knew what she was doing, he lifted the door, and she fixed one screw in the top hinge and another into the bottom one. The door hung loosely and she steadied it while he fixed the other screws.

Her hands were icy, but she was pleased that she'd been able to help him. Perhaps it was because Emma had just told her about his wife and young daughter. He was coping very well with what fate had dealt him. His three years of solitary sadness proved to her that not all men were unfaithful frauds, and that worthwhile love did exist.

When he finished, he tested the door and swung it back and forth. He was satisfied as it skimmed unhindered over the paving stones.

'Perfect!' Sara said. Looking up at a sky covered in grey clouds winging speedily above them, and she noted that daylight was fading fast. 'It looks like rain is on the way. Bye, Mr Crossley.'

After a moment of caution, his face relaxed. 'Alex, please. And thanks.'

'You're welcome. Glad I could help.' She turned away and hurried back into the warmth again.

A short time later, Sara was settled in her cheerful room. It looked over the back garden. The windows had flowery chintz curtains, and the room was decorated in various shades of lively yellow.

Glancing out, she saw there was a long narrow strip of vegetable garden behind the outhouse. There were dark outlines in one of the rows, presumably the last of cabbages or some other vegetable that had so far defied the cold of winter. A surrounding beech-tree hedge now only contained skeleton-like twigs and branches. Brown leaves were swirling like lost souls along the base of the hedge and drifting back and forth along the bordering pathway. It was the week before Christmas, and it wasn't the best time of year to be admiring the English countryside.

Emma straightened up and told herself she was glad she was here. It didn't matter if the countryside looked abandoned. She definitely had no reason to be fed up or disgruntled. Rod was past history and she felt no regret. People like Alex Crossley and Emma had survived much harder knocks than she'd ever known.

For a moment, she looked at Alex down below in the yard. He was gathering his tools and putting them back into his toolbox. She turned away and began to unpack her holdall.

2

When Sara entered the dining room, she took a measured look at her fellow visitors and sensed their mutual curiosity and anticipation. They'd all chosen to spend Christmas in this place, in this house. They'd meet every day for meals, and everyone hoped for the best. The other three were already sitting comfortably and looked up when she came in. She gave them a smile and said, 'Good evening: I'm Sara Holden.' She held out her hand to the closest one. He was a youngish man who looked pleased to see someone else of roughly his own age. He stood up and took her hand.

'Pleased to meet you. I'm Peter Terrell.'

The other man was tall, middle-aged, and had a fresh complexion and a salt-and-pepper moustasche. He stood up briefly and also took her outstretched hand. 'Roland Calderwood-Morris. This is my wife Veronica.'

Veronica smiled nervously and reached across the table to shake Sara's hand. She was overdressed for the countryside, with a pale pink ruffled blouse and too much fussy jewellery. Her pale grey eyes viewed Sara with interest. She was probably glad to see another woman.

Sara studied the others silently as she sat down on the high-backed chair clearly meant for her, because the place was empty and set with shiny cutlery and a white serviette.

Roland Calderwood-Morris was plainly used to being in charge. He lost no time in familiarizing himself. 'What do you do for a living, Miss Holden? Peter was just telling us that he's a banker in the city.'

'I'm a graphic designer in a small company situated on the outskirts of London.'

'Oh, one of these modern jobs, eh?

Can't say I understand much about advertising, computers or the like. Sometimes I think the world got on better without them before they came along.'

'You could say that about every new-fangled innovation. Stone Age man managed without the wheel, and later generations without the printing press, the steam engine, radio or television, but they improved and enriched people's lives when they did come along.' Sara wasn't going to be daunted by his forthright approach. 'What do you do?'

'Army. Retired. Been posted to a lot of outlandish and dangerous places in our time.' He flicked an invisible speck from his tweed jacket and checked his watch.

Sara sighed inwardly. That was all she needed to make a perfect Christmas — an ex-military man who loved punctuality and wanted to hog the conversation. She cautioned herself not to get preconceived ideas about him, or anyone else. It was a bad habit. She'd analyzed Alex's role, only to find he was just a next-door neighbour. Perhaps Calderwood-Morris was pleasant too, when you knew him better.

She was glad when Emma came in with a steaming soup tureen; not just because it silenced Roland for a while, but because she was hungry. Emma placed it in front of Veronica.

'Will you serve, please? Then I can get back to preparing the rest of the meal.'

Veronica nodded. She sat stiffly, holding out her hands for everyone's soup plate.

Sara was curious enough to ask, 'Were you with your husband on all these assignments and postings, Mrs Calderwood-Morris?'

The woman's voice was quiet but unwavering. 'Yes, whenever it was possible.'

'And did you enjoy it?'

Roland gave a gruff laugh and looked at his wife briefly. 'Why not?'

Sara wished he'd let his wife answer

for herself. 'Because I presume that moving around all the time isn't everyone's cup of tea.'

'If you marry a military man, you marry his job — but because you're a civilian, you'd probably find that hard to understand, Miss Holden.'

Trying not to get het up, she said, 'Sara, please.' The more rebellious side of her emotions took over and she continued, while not forgetting to empty her soup plate. 'Why should a wife automatically enjoy military life? Surely she's primarily your wife, and only secondly the wife of an army officer?'

Roland waved his hand vaguely in her direction. 'I agree that's how it should be. But when he reaches a certain rank, an aspiring officer always needs an understanding wife in the background; and that won't happen if she hates army life.' He held out his soup plate. 'I'd like another helping, my dear. Damned good soup, this.'

Sara decided to turn her attention to

the other visitor, Peter. She gave him an encouraging smile. 'Emma mentioned you've been here before? You must have enjoyed yourself, otherwise you wouldn't have come back.'

Eagerly he leaned forward. 'Yes. It was a first-class stay. The weather was much better in the summer of course. We went for long hikes across the moor every day. Didn't see another soul all day.' He asked hopefully, 'Do you like walking?'

Sara thought he looked like an eager puppy. His blond hair flopped onto his forehead and his expression was appealing. 'I'm not much of a serious walker. I just like the occasional stroll.'

'Oh, I see. Pity! There's no better way to enjoy nature.'

Sara smiled softly. 'Even so, I can't imagine hiking out in the moorlands in this kind of weather.'

Peter returned her smile. 'Definitely not as pleasant as in summer, but a dedicated walker doesn't mind bad weather. If you have the right clothes, you can forget about the disagreeable aspects. It makes you appreciate good cooking and a warm bed all the more when you get back.'

Roland swept his moustache upward with his index finger. 'That's the spirit, young man. Good to see someone with a bit of backbone. I'm surprised that you're a banker. Always believed they'd be the last people who wanted to get out into the fresh air. You'd have made a good soldier.'

Peter straightened his tie and looked self-conscious. 'I don't think so. I'm too independent. I don't like taking orders from other people; that's why I chose to work in a section of finance where I can make my own judgments about current market developments.'

Emma returned and cleared their soup plates. Sara reached forward for the jug of water in the centre of the table to fill her glass.

The rest of the meal went off quite well. Sara didn't rise to the bait every time Roland made a running comment that she didn't agree with. There was little point in contesting his opinions all the time. Perhaps he'd relax once he was more familiar with the other visitors. On the other hand, it was easy to empathize with Peter.

Towards the end of the meal, the Calderwood-Morrises announced they intended to watch a thriller in the lounge. Sara wondered what would happen if she or Peter wanted to watch something else. It might start World War Three.

After the older couple left the room, Peter lifted his eyebrows and said, 'I'm so glad you're here and I don't need to face Roland on my own every day.'

Sara laughed softly. 'Perhaps he'll improve in time.'

She was tired from the rush of getting away from her flat, and the journey, and was glad to leave the others and have an early night. She got ready, and as soon as she settled back onto the pillows with a paperback, she soon began to feel drowsy. The wind was howling outside, and she heard the branches of some trees near the house groaning in protest. Even though the sounds were completely foreign to her ears, she was warm, she was safe, she'd had plenty to eat, and she was tired. It wasn't long before she put out the bedside light and turned onto her side to have a dreamless sleep.

★   ★   ★

The next morning Sara stuck her arms out of the security and warmth of the bedclothes and stretched. Just for a moment she revelled in the knowledge that she didn't need to rush to work. Dappled sunshine struggled round the edges of the curtains and encouraged her to fling back the duvet and search for her slippers with her toes as she got up. Opening the curtains, she was pleased to find that the wind had dropped. It was quiet and calm. The trees were static this morning, and some weak rays of sunshine were trying their best to break through the clouds. There was a barely noticeable covering of frost on the ground, and the fields stretching behind the house looked like someone had sprinkled them with icing sugar.

Emma hadn't mentioned a definite time for breakfast, but when she looked at her watch, Sara realized she'd slept much longer than usual and wondered if she'd get any breakfast at all this morning. Washed and dressed, she found she was alone in the dining room. Emma must have heard her and came to check. She bustled in, wiping her hands on her apron.

'Did you sleep well?'

Sara smiled. 'Like a top. I presume I'm the last down for breakfast? I hope I haven't kept you from doing something else. I'm usually much earlier than this. The country air must be affecting me.'

'Don't worry about the time. You're welcome to help yourself in the kitchen if I've already cleared the table in here.

I leave it till about ten-thirty. After that it's up to you. The evening meal is more organized because of the cooking involved, but breakfast is very relaxed. What would you like? A cooked breakfast with all the trimmings, or something simpler?'

'Just some toast and coffee for me, please. That's what I always have.'

Emma tut-tutted. 'You should start the day with a decent meal. Well, there are a couple of varieties of homemade jam, local honey, and marmalade on the sideboard over there. Are you sure that's all you want?'

'Sure.'

Emma straightened her pearl necklace. 'What are you going to do today?'

'Nothing much. Perhaps I'll go for a walk and take a look around the village.' She looked at the empty chairs around the table. 'The others are already out?'

'Peter set out on one of his hikes with a packet of sandwiches a short while ago, so I presume he'll be out all day.

The major and his wife have gone off in their car. I think they intend to visit the cathedral in next market town, and to have a look around the shops. It's very picturesque. Most of the buildings in the square are still half-timbered, and the cathedral is ancient. At this time of year the shops are full of festive wares, and you're almost transported back to the middle ages when you wander through the old part of the town. I think there's even a Christmas market this year. I know the council has banned traffic from the area.'

'That sounds good. I'll go there before I leave.'

'Do that. I haven't seen the Christmas market yet, but I'm sure it's worth a look. Now let's get you your toast and coffee.' Emma bustled off and soon returned with a plate of piping-hot toast.

Sara plastered it with butter, which melted on the surface almost before she'd added some of Emma's delicious plum jam. As she sat munching her toast and reading the morning paper, left conveniently on the table, she enjoyed the fact that the house was so quiet. After a while she heard Emma upstairs, presumably checking the bedrooms and the bathroom. She had a feeling that she'd chosen the right place. She loved being with her parents for Christmas, but this was as good a replacement as she was likely to find, despite Roland — but perhaps even he would improve in time.

She decided to walk to the village and asked Emma for directions.

'You can't miss it. Just carry on to the right for about ten minutes. There aren't many houses between here and there. Alex's house is the next one along the road and then there are two others, further back off the road before you reach the village. There's not a lot to see when you get there, but I think it's a pretty place. We have a small grocer's, a newsagent's, a hairdresser, and a baker. We used to have a butcher until quite recently. He couldn't compete with the prices in the supermarket and works on the supermarket meat counter these days. The village shop also has some ready-packed meat, but no great variety. Take a look at the church. It's small and was built to stand the passing of time. You can't miss it. The lychgate is on the main road, opposite the newsagent's.'

3

A couple of minutes later, Sara was on her way. Suitably dressed, she felt comfortable and inhaled the cold air as she went along. Dappled rays of sunshine still fought their way through the branches of the bare trees and high hedges, and the frost had disappeared.

She soon reached what she presumed was Alex's house. It stood in the morning shadows and there was no sign of anyone at home. Out of interest, she studied it more carefully. It was a large modern house with simple lines and a large garden. A swing and climbing frame stood in one of the corners. There were tidy flowerbeds in their winter attire, and low evergreen bushes leading to a double garage on one side. She liked the look of it all.

When she reached the village, it was quiet. She met few people as she walked along. There were houses of various styles. Some of them had peeling Victorian stucco fronts, others were very modern bungalows with perfectly tended gardens, and there were even a couple of half-timbered homes lurching towards each other, sandwiched between narrow passage-ways. She bought some chocolate in the shop and then focussed her attention on the church. The lychgate needed oiling, but somehow that was part of its charm. On her way towards the church building, she passed gravestones cov-ered with lichen, and others that looked in danger of toppling over. The newer ones were further back beneath the surrounding dry-stone wall. Standing like soldiers in tidy rows, they looked better cared for. She reached the porch and turned the old-fashioned solid ring in the door. It gave way and she went inside.

It was empty and silent. Sara looked with interest at the various old features and edifices. The long, narrow windows with their pointed tops were a blaze of coloured glass. Even the weak winter sunshine was enough to set them alight. She was startled when she heard a sound from the vestry door on the side. Suddenly it opened and a man came in, unravelling a long woollen scarf from his neck. He looked at Sara and smiled. She noticed the dog collar and felt obliged to explain.

'Good morning, Vicar. My landlady suggested I take a look around your church. It's beautiful in a simple, unpretentious way.'

'Yes, I agree. I've been vicar here over twenty years, and when I come I still enjoy the colour and the sense of history. It is a pleasure to be responsible for this little community. You're staying locally? Where, if I may ask?'

'I'm staying with Emma, Emma Arber. Do you know her?'

His smile widened. 'I might have guessed. Yes, Emma mentioned she had a couple of visitors over Christmas. She's a wonderful tower of strength. I couldn't manage without her. I can always turn to Emma in an emergency, no matter what the problem is. She always finds a way to help, and she's so well-liked by everyone that she manages to get things done without ruffling too many feathers. I'd be lost without her. She's coming here this afternoon with another lady from the village to decorate the church for Christmas. Usually we have it all finished by now, but another job took priority and wrecked our timetable. The storm that raged across the whole country a couple of weeks ago damaged the roof of the community hall. We had to get it sorted out as soon as possible because we'd arranged to hold various Christmas celebrations there. The Women's Institute, the Pensioners' Club and the Historical Society were depending on using the rooms. People were expecting the church to be decorated for the beginning of Advent, but we had the decorating and cleaning in the community hall to finish off first. We're planning to get it done today though, in plenty of time for the Christmas services. If we don't, I'll face a barrage of disapproval and complaints. It's been a tight fit this year. I'm so grateful for the help of people like Emma. I can always count on them, whatever happens.'

Sara liked him. He had a kind face, friendly blue eyes, neatly cut grey hair, and a trim figure. He also had an endearing habit of leaning slightly towards his opposite number when he was talking, and it gave one the feeling he was genuinely interested in the topic under discussion. She remembered Emma mentioning that he was a widower, and she wondered how difficult it was to organize parish affairs without female help. There were probably numerous village events that functioned best with a supportive vicar's wife.

'Have you seen the tomb of Sir Richard de Lavely and his wife over there? He went to the Crusades. He promised if he returned that he would build a stone church, and he did. I expect there was only a wooden structure before then. He kept his promise, and when they died, both he and his wife found their final resting place here.'

He led the way to a shadowed corner near the entrance door where two life-sized effigies lay on a low tomb. With interest, Sara studied the clean-shaven stone features of the knight in his full armour and raised visor. He had his sword on one side, and next to him on the other side was his pious wife with her folded hands.

As added information, the vicar said, 'The dog curled up at his feet tells us that he almost certainly died in peace at home, so he was one of the lucky ones.'

Sara nodded. 'It's hard to imagine how ordinary people lived in those days. Your knight was better off than most people because he was born to wealth and a social position, but he still faced the prospect of catching awful diseases and coping with continual political strife.' She looked at her watch. 'I won't keep you any longer. I'm sure you have a lot to do. Perhaps we'll meet again before I leave.'

He gave a soft laugh. 'Parish work never ends, but I enjoy my work. If you're staying with Emma, perhaps I'll see you again. You're very, very welcome to come to the services and to join in with our Christmas celebrations.'

On the way home, Sara thought about the contrast between where she lived in the town and this quiet village. She did know some of her neighbours, but most of them only by name. They greeted each other in passing but rarely conversed with each other. Her downstairs neighbour was the only one she knew quite well. In this village she imagined that no one could live anonymously unless they had a very thick skin or were a dedicated recluse.

Lunch wasn't part of the arrangement, but Sara seldom ate at that time anyway, so she didn't miss it. Back at

Emma's she asked if she could make herself a cup of tea, and then settled down with her paperback in the lounge. It was at the back of the house, and an occasional wayward ray of sunshine strayed into the room now and then.

Emma popped her head round the door. 'I'm going to pick Katie up from school later on, but I've arranged to meet someone first to decorate the church for Christmas. Do you need anything? Don't forget to take your key if you go out.'

Sara looked up. 'No, I'll remember.' She paused, struck by a sudden idea. 'I don't want to seem pushy, but would you like some extra help? I met your vicar this morning. He told me you intended to decorate the church. I'd enjoy helping. I'm not doing anything special, and . . . '

Emma's expression lightened. 'That would be lovely. There's only Janet and me, and we have more than enough to do. We always turn off the church heating to save on the energy bill during the week, so it's not exactly agreeable work in the cold. I thought we might even have to break off today because of the cold, and finish it tomorrow. It'll make all the difference if you come to help.'

Sara got up and closed her book. 'Willingly! I've never done anything similar before, so I hope I can help, and not cause extra problems. What about the evening meal? Will you manage that too?'

'Oh, I've prepared everything in advance, and only have to cook the vegetables when I get back. I always have one eye on the clock.' She paused. 'What did you think of our vicar? Paul's a nice man, isn't he?'

'What an appropriate name for a vicar! Yes, I liked him. He was very welcoming and friendly.'

Satisfied, Emma nodded. 'We're lucky to have someone like Paul. I'll get my coat.'

'Shall we go by car? If you have to pick Katie up from school, and also decorate the church in the cold, you might be glad to drive home afterwards and not have to walk.'

Emma shrugged. 'I'm used to it. I expect Alex would drop me off on his way home, but it's up to you.'

'Alex?'

'He's promised to bring us a tree for the church. We always have one to the side of the entrance.'

'Oh, I see.'

'If we go now, I'll have lots of time to do something before I have to pick Katie up from school.'

Sara followed her out of the room, put on her coat, wrapped a scarf around her neck and slid into her thickest boots again. She remembered that it had been cold in the church that morning, and it wasn't likely to be warmer in the afternoon. Emma joined her with a basket full of wire cutters, gardening wire, and various other items she knew from experience that she might need. Sara searched her pocket for the car keys and they were soon on their way.

* ★ ★

The church was empty when they got there. Emma explained what they had to do. There was a big pile of fir branches heaped in a corner near the main doorway. They smelt fresh and strong. Emma and Sara began to strip the branches and join them together into a long garland by winding the wire around a central stem. Sara was glad Emma had thought of gardening gloves, otherwise she'd have ended up with extremely dirty and resin-covered hands. She'd never done anything comparable before, but she soon got the hang of it, and before long they were both busy producing long garlands of fir to loop along the walls between the windows.

They'd been busy for a while when another woman, a bit younger, than Emma arrived. She pulled off her scarf and was clearly surprised to see Sara, but she smiled and came towards them.

'Hello! We have another helper.

44

That's good. And I see you've already made a start.'

Emma explained who Sara was and introduced them to each other. Sara learned that Janet lived in the village and was married to the local policeman. 'Janet is one of our stalwarts. She's always willing and ready to help.'

Janet smiled. 'That's the pot calling the kettle black, isn't it? No one around here does more church work than Emma. It's very kind of you to help, Sara, if you're on holiday.'

'I'm enjoying it. Usually my mother has already organized our Christmas decorations before I get home. This reminds me how much I used to enjoy it.'

Janet asked Emma, 'Do you want me to help with the garlands, or shall I start to hang them in place and finish off the niches? I'm worried about bringing the poinsettias in just yet. I've fetched them from the garden centre and they're really impressive, but they're not going to like the cold in here. It's really chilly, and I just heard there's a forecast of snow showers in the next couple of days. The shop wrapped the plants in newspaper to insulate them from the cold during the journey, but somehow I don't think that'll help much if we leave them here till the Christmas services. They're outside in the car.'

'Could you keep them somewhere at home, and then bring them over on Christmas Eve? You're getting visitors over Christmas, aren't you? Will they be in the way?'

'No. That's a good idea. I can put them in the conservatory. It's not too warm in there, and they'll get plenty of light.'

'Well pop home with them then, before you start here.' Emma looked at her watch. 'It's not quite time to fetch Katie yet, so I'll carry on with Sara till it's time to go. You do whatever you like when you come back. With Sara's help, we're already well on our way.'

Janet nodded and fixed her scarf with a secure knot again. 'Good idea! I'll be back in a couple of minutes.'

When she returned, the three women worked in companionship, and Sara enjoyed the relaxed and friendly atmosphere. Janet asked her about her job and where she came from, and the other two women gossiped about the forthcoming Christmas get-together of the Women's Institute and some of the other village happenings. By the time Emma paused and went off to pick up her little charge, they'd made very good progress with the fir garlands. Janet had already finished a section of the walls, hanging them in loops beneath the windows. The smell of pine already filled the old building. Sara could now well imagine how lovely a poinsettia in each window niche with a thick red candle, and resting on a layer of lush fir, would look.

'We usually add some bells to the garlands,' Janet said. 'They're over there in that box. Did Emma mention if Paul wanted us to decorate the font this year? I think it looked fantastic last year. I don't think we have a christening this Christmas though, so it may not be necessary.'

'I don't remember Emma mentioning a christening, but she did mention a crib and a Christmas tree.'

'Yes. I think she's persuaded Alex to get us the tree this year. Hopefully the contents of the crib are waiting for us in their box in the vestry. Paul promised to bring it over from the vicarage today.'

'I met him here when I was looking around this morning,' Sara said. 'So perhaps that's what he was doing.'

Some voices drifted closer, and the door opened to reveal a little girl. Emma was close behind. Katie was a pretty five-year-old with ash-blond curly hair and bright blue eyes. She was warmly dressed in jeans, a down jacket and thick winter boots. She tugged off her bright red woollen bonnet and scarf and looked excitedly around at all the activity. Her glance paused when she saw Sara. Emma explained who she was.

Sara said, 'Hello, Katie. You've come to help?'

The little girl looked excited and nodded.

'It would be a great help if you could unpack the crib with Sara,' Emma suggested, 'and make sure the figures are nice and clean. The vicar is coming soon. He's getting a bale of straw from Mr Booth, the farmer. Know who I mean?'

Katie nodded vigorously.

'Once we've arranged the hay around the floor next to the altar, we'll bring the crib in, and then you can help to place the figures. Show Sara where everything is. You helped me to unpack the figures last year, so you already know how careful you have to be with them.'

With an earnest expression, and without further ado, Katie nodded and trotted off down the aisle to the doorway to the vestry.

Sara asked, 'Are you sure? I don't mind helping with the garlands if you want to supervise Katie and the crib.'

'No, carry on. Katie will enjoy explaining all the various figures, I expect. She's a clever little thing, and I'm always surprised what a good memory she has.'

Sara pulled off the rough gloves and followed Katie. When she entered the vestry, the little girl was already trying to open a very large cardboard box. It was standing next to a waist-high wooden construction that was meant to represent the stable at Bethlehem. The simple form was squat and stumpy and open on one side. It looked like it had been constructed out of old bits of planks. The narrow roof was covered with dusty straw. It looked a bit grimy, but Sara mused that the original stable in Bethlehem hadn't looked any better.

'Gosh, that stable looks like the real thing, doesn't it? How many figures are there?'

Katie eyed her shyly for a moment and then decided this strange woman was okay. Emma clearly liked her, so she felt quite happy and confident. 'I've never counted them, but there are two shepherds and a boy shepherd, some lambs, a donkey, the three kings, and Mary, Joseph and the baby Jesus.' She was busy with her fingers. 'That's about twelve!'

'Where's the crib?'

Katie pointed. 'Over there under that blanket.'

'Right. We'll open the box and unpack everything together. Do you know where to find a duster, in case we need one?'

Confidently, Katie got up from her knees and went to a nearby cupboard. She reached up and wrestled with the door handle. When it was open, it revealed a bucket and several other items for cleaning, including a hand brush and some fluffy-looking dusters. She took one and brought it back.

Sara pulled off the tape sealing the box, and they began to extract the figures from their coverings of protective paper. To Sara they seemed quite large. Not life-sized, but even someone sitting at the back of the church would be able to see them easily.

They handled them carefully, lying them next to each other on the floor. They emerged from their coverings one by one and didn't need much dusting, but Katie and Sara dusted them anyway. Sara could tell that Katie was gradually feeling happier in her company. Her eyes sparkled as she chatted about the figures, what had happened last year and what their role was in the nativity scene.

'We're doing a nativity play in our class in my school too.'

Sara nodded. 'Yes, Emma told me. Are you going to be in it?'

Katie's lower lip jutted slightly. 'Yes, I'm an angel. I wanted to be Mary, but our teacher, Miss Butler, said that because I've only just started school, I'll have to wait. Perhaps I'll be Mary next year.'

Sara tried to show the right amount of understanding. 'I'm sure you'd make a great Mary, but I expect there are a lot of bigger girls who've been waiting to be Mary ever since they started school. Once they move to the upper school, younger ones will have a better chance.'

Katie eyed her carefully. 'That's what my daddy told me too. Would you like to come?'

Sara didn't hesitate long. 'Yes, but will your teacher allow me in?'

'Yes, Miss Butler told us to invite anyone we know. Mostly parents and grandparents come, but they allow other people, like Emma, too if they want to.'

A sudden draught flowed over them when Alex stuck his head round the door. He was clearly surprised to see Sara kneeling together with his daughter, and he appraised her with more than just mild interest in his eyes. There was something hidden in their depths, and it gave her a giddy sense of pleasure. Sara wished she knew what he was thinking at that moment and whether he felt as confused as she did. He hesitated before he finally smiled and joined them. Sara's heart seemed to skip a beat, and she felt a lurch of excitement as he neared them.

4

Alex's daughter flew into his arms. He lifted her high above his head, stroked the hair out of her face, and then kissed her forehead. 'How's my princess?'

Sara felt a lump in her throat. They were clearly a very close, loving unit. It was hard to imagine they needed anyone, or anything, else.

Over Katie's shoulder he met her eyes and said, 'I'm surprised to see you here, Sara.'

'Emma told me about the decorating and I offered to help.'

'And I see the two of you have been given the paramount job of getting the stable and the crib ready?'

Katie's eyes sparkled. 'We've almost finished, haven't we, Sara? Have you brought the Christmas tree, Daddy? Emma said you would.'

He laughed softly. 'Yes. I'm just going

to put it in its stand. When you've finished here, you can come and help me decorate it with stars.'

Katie clapped her hands excitedly. 'Emma's going to spread the straw near the altar so we can fetch the crib. I know where the baby Jesus goes, but I'm not sure about all the rest.'

Alex looked over her head at Sara and smiled. He let Katie slide back down to the floor. 'Emma will tell you. I'll come and help you carry the heavy parts like the stable if you tell me you're ready.'

He was almost through the door when Katie called after him, 'Daddy, don't forget you have to make me a costume for the nativity play. I gave you the note from Miss Butler, remember?'

He looked back at them, and from his expression Sara could tell he was worried about how to manage that task. He smiled half-heartedly and nodded silently. Being a single father clearly had its snags and impediments.

Sara and Katie carried on and even had time to clean some dust off the makeshift stable with the hand-brush, being careful not to dislodge any of the straw roof. Paul, the vicar, arrived with a large bale of straw. He beamed when he found Sara with the others.

'What a pleasant surprise. I didn't expect to see you here again today, Sara. It's extremely kind of you to help. How are you, Katie? Everything okay? Good day at school today?'

Katie nodded. With her lips pouting she said, 'But I didn't get the part of Mary.'

'Oh! Well, we did warn you, didn't we? That's the star part. All the girls want to be Mary. Never mind. You'll be chosen one day, I'm sure. You can impress the others in your class by telling them you helped us with the church decorations. No one else from your class has ever done that before.'

Katie tilted her head to the side. 'Okay! I'll tell Laura that if she starts boasting about being one of the shepherds, and making fun because I'm just an angel.'

Paul squatted down and looked her seriously in the face. 'Katie, what would the nativity play be without the angel? There's more than one shepherd, but there's only one angel, isn't there?'

Her expression brightened. 'I hadn't thought of that.'

He got up. 'I'll spread some straw and then help you carry the figures through from the vestry and arrange them. Then we'll see how we can help the others.'

Once Paul spread the straw over an area on one side of the altar and he'd positioned the figures, he looked at his watch, frowned and suddenly remembered a previous engagement. 'Heavens! I promised to call and see Ted Butler this afternoon. He's been housebound with bronchitis for a couple of weeks and his wife says he's getting short-tempered. I thought a game of dominos would cheer him up.'

From where she was standing, busy

helping Janet, Emma chuckled when she heard him. She shook her head. 'You promise too many people too much. But there's no point in trying to stop you, is there?' The two of them eyed each other like people who understood each other blind.

Sara noticed that Alex was still struggling with the Christmas tree. The rest of the church already looked quite beautiful. The colour of the fir, and the splashes of red candles and golden bells, transformed the cold stonework. The church glowed with the message of Christmas. The women had put wreaths of holly with red berries on the heads of the knight and his wife. It made them look festive and quite grand. The pungent smell of the fir from the decorative garlands and the other greenery filled the small building with its own special magic.

Paul wandered down the aisle towards the door, looking around and saying how splendid everything looked. Katie skipped her way down the aisle to join her father and stood watching until he was finally satisfied with how he'd positioned the tree. He finally managed to extract himself from underneath the lower branches and felt happy it wouldn't collapse. He ran his hands through his thick hair and brushed his clothes free of the unwanted needles.

He explained to Katie, 'It's okay now, but I had to shorten it twice. Once because it was too big and the tip brushed the ceiling, and then a second time because it wasn't straight.' He took a step back to admire the result.

Paul laughed. 'You'd never believe how often I've heard stories about people's disasters with their Christmas trees.' Looking very satisfied, he disappeared through the door while saying over his shoulder, 'The tree looks brilliant, Alex.'

Janet and Emma came over. Janet remarked, 'It's a lovely tree, Alex. How did you know what size?'

His eyes twinkled. 'I guessed. The eye

of an engineer! I had to leave the car's hatch open to get it here.'

Emma hurried them along. 'Once we have the stars on the tree, we'll be finished. That's lovely. I thought we'd have to come back tomorrow.'

Janet and Emma left them to arrange the stars and fetched brooms to clear the debris. Alex picked up the box of straw stars from the side. 'If you two tackle the lower branches, I'll stick some on the top part.'

'Daddy, don't forget that the biggest one goes right at the top.'

'I won't.' He pulled the stepladder into position and grabbed a handful of stars. Looking down at Sara, who was busy hanging stars with Katie, he commented, 'Considering you're only a visitor on holiday, I'm still surprised that you give up your time to help us.'

Sara fixed one and said, 'If I hadn't come, I'd have only read a book. I'm enjoying it. I explained to Emma and Janet just now that I haven't had the chance to do much Christmas decorating for years. By the time I get home to visit my parents, it's all finished. I never bother very much in my own flat because it's not worth it, although I do have an artificial tree with coloured lights.'

'I didn't bother much after my wife died either, but Katie wants more every year now, don't you, love? I can't get away with doing nothing anymore.'

Katie giggled. 'And don't forget my costume, Daddy. I want to be the best angel ever!'

He ran his hand over his face, and Sara met his worried glance. 'I'd forgotten all about it,' he said. 'I'll have to put my thinking cap on sharpish, won't I?'

Sara didn't hesitate. 'Would you like me to make it? I think it'd be fun, and Katie can help when she comes to Emma's after school.' She thought for a moment. 'We'll need some strong wire, some kind of white material for the dress, then strong white paper for the wings; and if we can get them, it'd be great to have some white feathers to cover them with. We'd also need some gold bits for the trimmings. Emma can tell me where to buy things.'

He viewed her silently. His dark eyes were full of unspoken questions. 'I'd be eternally grateful of course, because I don't have the slightest clue where to start, and both grandmothers are tied up at the moment. My parents are on holiday in Florida, and my wife's mother is due to keep a hospital appointment any day now. She's worried about that, and I don't want to trouble her. Are you sure?'

'I wouldn't offer otherwise.' She squatted down. 'Shall we make it together, Katie? Will you help?'

Katie nodded fiercely, and she had spots of red excitement on her cheeks.

For a brief second, Alex studied Sara's face and wondered if she was just another one of those women he'd met since Susan's death who were driven by pure emotional motivation. They usually declared they wanted to help him with Katie, but they were actually hoping to manoeuvre him into a corner. On the other hand, Sara wasn't going to be around very long, so it wasn't likely that that was her objective. She seemed to be down-to-earth and helpful, so he decided there was no reason for him to be sceptical.

'It'd be a big weight off my mind,' he said. 'I can handle a hammer, but creating an angel is very daunting, so I'll accept your offer with thanks. Naturally I'll fork out for any expense involved — just tell me what you spend.'

Emma joined them. She'd caught the end of the conversation. 'I'll ask Ted Booth to give us some feathers,' she murmured quietly in Sara's ear. 'He'll be selling geese for Christmas, so he'll have plenty to spare. I've an old white bedsheet you can cut up for making the dress. Yes, thick paper would be better for the wings than wobbly cloth.'

Katie jumped up and down. 'When can we start?'

Sara smiled. 'Tomorrow, if you like. But it depends on whether I've found all we need by then.'

Emma looked at her watch. 'It's definitely too late to do anything else today, so don't worry about that any more, Katie. Would you like to come back with us for a meal, Alex?'

He shook his head. 'You have enough work with your visitors. Katie and I will make pasta and a tomato sauce. One of our specialities.' He picked up his hip-length coat from a nearby pew and gestured to his daughter. 'Let's go.'

Katie zipped up her anorak again, rushed to find her hat and scarf, and put them back on. She hurried across to thrust her hand into her father's and shouted back over her shoulder, 'See you tomorrow, Sara!'

The three women began shoving the debris into plastic bags and admiring the results of their efforts around them. When they finished, Emma left the other two to go out through the vestry so that she could turn off the lights.

Sara and Janet stood waiting for her outside the main entrance. Daylight had almost disappeared. Sara asked, 'What about locking the door?'

'As far as I know, it's never locked,' Janet said. 'Paul insists there's nothing valuable or interesting to pinch, but there are always vandals just looking for kicks. My husband, Randall, has tried to persuade him, but Paul thinks having the church open day and night is more important. We're a small village and everyone knows everyone else. There isn't any great danger, but there are the candlesticks on the altar, for example. I think they're silver, plated with gold. They'd interest a thief.' Sara nodded. 'Perhaps my hubby will convince Paul one day. It'd mean extra journeys for Paul, of course. Perhaps that's why he wants it to stay like it is. He already has too much to do, and is always busy.'

'Emma told me that too. She mentioned that he tries to compensate for not having a wife to handle lots of things a vicar's wife usually does.'

'Emma and Paul's wife were good friends, and Emma's been a tremendous support for him since she died. He tries not to bother her too much, because he says it's his responsibility, not hers.'

Emma came around the corner and they said goodbye to Janet at the lychgate. They breathed in the cold air as they went to her car.

Emma sighed softly. 'It was good of you to come. We would've been there tomorrow again without your help.'

Sara started the engine and said, 'I enjoyed it, honestly.'

The journey through the village was short. The roads were quiet, and a full moon lit up the trees bordering the verges as they passed. Lights were glowing in the windows of the houses and cottages. Glancing briefly, Sara saw that nearly everyone had some kind of Christmas decoration: coloured lights, candles, or illuminated seasonal figures glowed behind the dark glass. The road was sprinkled with the luminescent glitter of frost on the ground. Minutes later they reached their destination.

Parking neatly, Sara noticed there was also a pricey car parked alongside the kerb that she hadn't seen before. Emma noticed it immediately. 'Oh, Ken! I didn't know he was going to call. Come and meet him.'

Sara didn't have the heart to refuse.

★   ★   ★

Ken was tall with black curly hair, bright blue eyes and a lazy smile. He appraised Sara carefully when his mother introduced her, and held out his hand. 'Pleased to meet you.'

Sara took it and he held it in hers a mite too long. 'Hello.' She noticed the sleek haircut, classy clothes and his air of confidence, probably the result of a large bank account. He owned an expensive car, and she wondered briefly why his mother was dependent on help from a neighbour to do her repairs and had to take in visitors to supplement her income if he was that affluent.

His eyes twinkled. 'If I'd known my mother had such an attractive visitor, I'd have called earlier. But now I have an incentive to call again soon.'

His mother smiled. 'Stop trying to impress Sara. She knows how to handle types like you. Are you staying for something to eat?'

He smiled. 'Can't, I'm afraid. I have to take a client out for a meal. I just popped in on my way because I haven't seen you for a while. Everything okay?'

Hiding her disappointment, Emma said, 'Yes, okay.'

He nodded. 'Good. I haven't forgotten that I promised to get you a Christmas tree. There's a chap selling them on the corner of the high street; I'll ask him to pick a good one.'

She nodded. 'Well don't forget. I'm depending on you. I can't keep asking Alex to do things for me.'

He grabbed her around her plump waist. 'Stop worrying. If I say I'll get one, I'll get one.'

Emma couldn't stop her smile. 'If you forget, I'll nag you for the rest of your life. Coming on Christmas Day? Or have you other plans again?'

'I promised Lydia and Michael to go to their Christmas Day party — that's if I don't go to the south of France with friends for the holiday. Nothing's been definitely settled yet. If Sara's here, I might even upend my plans and come after all.'

Sara felt awkward. She guessed Emma was disappointed to find that she was so far down her son's list of obligations. Sara had met other men like him — men who often got their priorities wrong; men whose thought-lessness sometimes hurt the very people who did the most for them. They were usually charming and intelligent, often very successful and very accomplished, but they hadn't figured out what counted in life. Emma was a lovely down-to-earth person. Her son was flamboyant. Either Ken followed his father, or his working environment had made him what he was. It was quite likely he'd fallen into the habit of pretending to be what he wasn't because of his job.

She felt obliged to say something. 'I can't honestly imagine celebrating in the south of France at Christmas, but it takes all sorts to make a world.' She looked at her watch. 'I need a shower. Nice to meet you, Ken.' Without waiting for a reply, she left.

In the hall she met Peter, who was just coming back from his day of hiking. His face lightened when he saw her. He was suitably dressed in hiking kit and thick walking boots. Honest as he was, he admitted, 'I'm glad to be back. I had a great day and saw some lovely scenery, but it's a lot colder than when I was here in the summer.'

Sara paused. 'I'm sure it is. Aren't you afraid of getting lost, or having some kind of accident? Especially when you're on your own.'

'I have a hand-held GPS device. I know from my last visit that it works everywhere on the moor. Emma usually asks me where I'm heading, just in case, and I tell her.'

'That's very sensible. Are you planning another walk for tomorrow?'

'Yes, but not such a long one. I normally do it like that. One whole day walking, and the next a shorter distance.' He paused. 'If you're not doing anything tomorrow and would like some fresh air, you're welcome to join me.'

'I've promised a little girl I'd help her make a costume for her school's nativity play. I'm planning to drive to town to look for what I need. She's going to be an angel, and we intend to make a start on it tomorrow afternoon when she comes home from school.'

He was silent for a moment. 'That'd be Katie? She's a sweet little thing, isn't she? If you like, we could walk into town together to do your shopping and get some exercise. If we take a short cut across the moor, it's fairly direct. Provided that we start out after a leisurely breakfast, we can walk there and be back easily by lunchtime. Some fresh air will do you good.' He waited expectantly.

Sara gave in and laughed softly. 'Okay! But only if you promise not to sprint along! I'm not used to walking long distances.'

He beamed. 'Good! I promise you that I don't expect military standards of so many miles an hour. I'll leave that kind of thing up to Major Calderwood-Morris.'

She nodded. 'I think we'd better get ourselves spruced up now though, don't you? We might be asked to stand to attention so that Roland can make an inspection before we sit down for our meal.'

He shrugged and laughed. 'If he was in the army all his life, he can't change the way he acts or thinks anymore. We have to make allowances.'

'You're probably right, but I feel sorry for his wife. She looks like she gave up making her own decisions a long time ago. I wish she'd show more independence.' Sara turned towards the stairs. Peter bent to remove his boots.

Once she was in her room, she thought how quickly and pleasantly her first day had gone. She'd enjoyed helping in the church. It had put her into the right mood for Christmas and she'd met some nice people into the bargain. She sent her sister and her parents some quick encouraging SMSs but didn't mention Rod or where she was, just that she was having a good time.

5

The next morning Sara edged her way between the cold bodies of the cars parked in front of the house and hoisted her small backpack into place. She was glad she'd included a sturdy pair of shoes in her luggage and a warm anorak. She felt comfortable.

Peter looked at her and said, 'Ready? If I walk too fast, just tell me.'

Sara nodded and fell into step. They walked companionably through the village and past the municipal playing field. Not long after, they climbed a wooden stile that had seen better days in a bordering hedge, and walked along the side of a ploughed field until they were in open spaces covered in winter gorse and heather.

She asked, 'I presume walking is your main hobby?'

'Yes. Just as some people get hooked

on jogging, my passion for walking has increased with the passing of time. Perhaps it's because of the contrast to my sedentary office job. I usually go somewhere different every time. I'd been planning to go to Spain now with my girlfriend, but we broke up a little while ago, so I forgot that idea, and left it too late to organize something else. I remembered how much we'd enjoyed staying with Emma and decided to come back here instead.'

'I'm sorry about your girlfriend, but I can understand how you feel. I broke up with my boyfriend not long ago too. A coincidence, isn't it — you and me with the same kind of recent history. Are you sorry? I'm not. He was having an affair behind my back and I'm glad I found out in time.'

'My girlfriend said we were in a rut, and when she told me she'd had enough, she didn't give us a chance to turn things around. She just said there was no point in going on and we didn't have enough going for us anymore.'

'How long were you together?'

'Almost two years. I still haven't adjusted properly. I wouldn't have minded quite so much if I hadn't heard she's already found someone else.'

'Well, it certainly wasn't the love of a lifetime if she found someone else so easily, was it?'

'I suppose not. But on top of breaking up, when you've been together that long, you often lose touch with other friends. I don't know about you, but I haven't had enough courage to get in touch with old friends again in case they feel I'm just using them. Making new ones takes time, and so I tend to float around, feeling sorry for myself, and doing nothing. I sent friends Christmas and birthday cards but didn't make the effort to keep in touch personally. That was a mistake. I've been thinking about contacting some of them and explaining that Pam and I have split up, but I keep putting it off. I'm still hoping she'll change her mind.'

'I wouldn't bet on it if she has

someone new. You should try to pick up your old friendships again. If you know where they hang out, you could try to meet them there by chance. It's worth a try, isn't it? What about making new friends in the hiking community?'

He grinned briefly. 'Hiking is a hobby for individuals. Even if you meet people with the same interests, you rarely do more than share a drink with them in the evening before you go to bed. Walking with my girlfriend was an ideal situation. It was shared pleasure. There are hiking organizations, but meetings are often talks about someone's most recent walk with a film or slides. Not for me, I'm afraid!'

'I haven't told many people about my breakup yet either, but I will after Christmas. It isn't the end of the world. It's a chance for a new beginning; something better perhaps.'

'You didn't want to spend Christmas with your family or friends?'

Sara shrugged. 'I didn't tell anyone I'd be spending it here. My parents are on a cruise, and my sister Liz had already planned to visit her boyfriend's family. If I'd told friends, it might have generated an automatic invitation, and I didn't want that. I don't mind, though; in fact it's turning out to be a lot better than I expected. Didn't you want to spend it with your family?'

'My parents died in a car crash a couple of years ago. I have a sister, but she lives in Greece, and she'd already planned to spend it with her husband's family. She'll be cross when she finds out I was on my own. I didn't want to tell her because she'd have changed her plans just for my sake.'

Sara nodded and thrust her hands deeper into her pocket. 'Exactly why I didn't mention it to Liz or anyone else either.'

Nearby, some startled birds broke their cover and took to the sky. For a while all they heard was the sound of their feet crunching the dry bracken still half-frozen from the previous night as they walked along. The day remained overcast, and the wind was driving the clouds before it in the sky above them. She felt comfortable with Peter. They'd both faced the same kind of let-down recently. She liked him; he was honest and straightforward.

He pointed out various features in the landscape, and also some wildlife that she wouldn't have noticed if she'd been on her own as they went along. He was clearly interested and knowledge-able about nature locally. Sara was surprised how quickly the time went, and how soon she spotted the silhouette of the town. As they drew closer, the sounds of civilization grew noticeably louder.

Once they reached the road leading into the town, the traffic soon overtook them, and a short time later they were in the middle of harassed-looking shoppers who were hurrying from shop to shop. The town centre was particu-larly busy, and they asked several people where they could find a handicraft shop before someone gave them the right information. It was down a side street, and today it was just as busy as all the other shops. People were buying things to make Christmas decorations, or to create beautiful packaging.

Sara soon found some gold-coloured ribbon, some twisted gold cord, some large sheets of thick white paper, a reel of strong wire, and some glue. Emma had already given her an old white bedsheet that morning before they left. She stuffed her purchases, apart from the rolled paper, into her backpack. Peter took charge of that.

When they were back outside, Peter said, 'You seem to have a definite idea of how to make this costume.'

She nodded. 'Making the wings will be the difficult part. The frame has to be strong enough, and I'd like to cover them in feathers — if we can manage it. I think I'm going to have more fun than Katie.'

Peter grinned. 'Let's have a cup of coffee before we go back — if we can find an empty table. Do you want to go by bus? Or shall we walk?'

She laughed softly. 'I think you'd be very disappointed if we went by bus, wouldn't you? Actually, I enjoyed our walk. It wasn't as strenuous as I expected. We'll walk.'

After a welcome cup of coffee and a sandwich, they went way back through the busy throng and passed the local Christmas market on the way. The cobblestone square had wooden stands positioned all around its perimeter. They offered local arts and crafts, all kinds of stocking fillers, sweets, candles and hot food. Everything was waiting to be bought and every purchase waiting to be celebrated with some mulled wine. The whole scene was coming to life because it was gloomy, dismal weather and the sky hadn't brightened much all day. Although the half-timbered buildings in the background were alight with Christmas decorations, the lighting on the stalls eclipsed them brilliantly. The whole effect was incredibly Christmassy. Strings of coloured lights on the stalls, the smell of cinnamon and spices from stands offering mulled wine, and the sound of Christmas carols created a perfect atmosphere.

By the time they got back to Emma's, daylight was fading and the house was gradually slipping into darkness. Sara heard Katie's high-pitched voice as soon as they came into the hallway. She must be home early. It wasn't long after two o'clock.

Katie rushed down the corridor towards them, viewing the roll in Peter's hand excitedly. 'Is that for the costume?'

'Yes, it is. What are you doing here? You're early, aren't you?'

Taking off her outdoor clothes, Sara took the roll from Peter and saw he was looking for a chance to discreetly disappear.

'Miss Butler wanted to rehearse some of the play with the main characters.'

'Did Emma know?'

'Yes, otherwise I would have had to stay until school finished as usual. I told Emma yesterday on the way to the church.'

'I see. So are you ready?'

'Of course. Emma has a plastic bag full of goose feathers. They're so fluffy and white. Emma doesn't want me to touch them yet, because she's afraid they'll fly around the whole room.'

Sara laughed. 'Well, I can understand that. They have a habit of taking off under their own steam if they're given the chance. We don't need them today. I'm going to ask Emma if we can use her sewing machine, and we'll start off by making your dress.'

Emma showed them into a small parlour at the back of the house. 'You can leave it all lying around. I won't bother to tidy the room until it's all finished. My sewing machine's very basic but I think it'll suit. Like some tea, Sara?'

'That'd be lovely, but don't bother if you're busy!'

'No bother. If Katie's with you, it gives me a chance to make some cake.'

After she left, Sara declared, 'Jump onto this chair, Katie! I'll measure you. We'll sew a straight tube, leaving a hole for your head, and add some wide sleeves. I bought some gold cord today and you can use that for a belt.'

Climbing promptly onto an old-fashioned dining chair, Katie enquired, 'How will I hold the wings up?'

'Hopefully, if things work out, the wings will go through slits in your dress at the back, and the ends will be attached to elastic loops that go round your arms inside the dress. I want that part to be out of sight inside your dress if possible.'

Katie jumped up and down and nodded.

Sara smiled. 'Stand still so that I can measure you properly, then you can help me pin the bits together after I've cut the dress out.'

* * *

By Thursday afternoon the costume was finished. Peter had even helped to stick on a couple of layers of goose feathers one evening. That was a great help because it was very time-consuming. The feathers needed enough glue to fix them in place, but too much glue just messed everything up and made the next layer more difficult to fix. Sara found she needed to let one row of feathers dry before she did the next one. Even quick-drying glue needed time to harden. She lost count of the number of feathers they'd glued, but it looked good and it had been fun. Alex checked their progress every day when he picked Katie up.

Their eyes met and they smiled at each other knowingly. Katie protested whenever he said it was time to go home. Some days he looked tired, and Sara had a ridiculous feeling of wanting to cheer him up.

With hidden laughter in his eyes, he remarked, 'I didn't think making an angel would turn Katie into a little tyrant. It's all she talks about anymore.'

Sara wondered briefly what sort of a man he'd been before he'd met and married his wife. 'She wants a pretty costume and she's made a great effort. She's a good worker.' Sara gave Katie a quick hug and the little girl beamed. Sara had grown to like her very much. She was a lively soul and loved to talk nonstop about school and her best friend Laura. She talked about her Dad often too, and Sara thought it was very touching how concerned she was about him. Sara already knew that they had a miniature artificial Christmas tree this year, with silver branches and coloured lights.

Katie explained, 'I persuaded Dad to buy it last year even though he didn't want to.'

Sara had seen it in the window when she walked past. Katie had gone a step further this year and persuaded him to make some red and green paper chains on the weekend. They now decorated the living-room walls.

Ignoring his daughter's protests, Alex finally gathered her up into his arms and said, 'Young lady, it's time to go. Tomorrow is a big day, and you need to be in bed on time for once.'

Katie giggled and he smiled indulgently. 'Emma said she'll bring your costume to the school in plenty of time for you to change into it. I'll be there to see your moment of glory too.' He looked up at Sara. 'I hope you'll come too and see the results of all your hard work?'

Sara nodded and smiled. 'Wouldn't miss it.'

He paused. 'Would you like me to pick you up? I know Emma's going early. Not just because of Katie's costume, but also because they have mince pies, and tea or coffee afterwards. I expect you aren't surprised to hear Emma volunteered to help.'

Sara tilted her head to the side. 'Emma gets landed with all kinds of jobs, and I suspect she's probably never learned to say no. She seems to thrive on it all, and she doesn't mind. If it's not taking you out of your way, I'll be grateful for a lift. I'm not sure where the school is yet. I was thinking about walking, but a lift isn't a bad idea at this time of year.'

'Right. I'll be here at roughly four-fifteen. The play is supposed to start at four-thirty.'

'Fine!'

With a departing gesture, he threw a giggling Katie over his shoulder and left.

★ ★ ★

It hadn't rained since Sara had arrived, although it was very cold and now rain was forecast. Christmas was almost here, and windows were decorated with fairy lights and twinkling shapes. People weren't happy about the perpetual stream of Christmas carols on the radio, but if asked they were honest enough to admit they also contributed to making it a special time. Emma insisted her visitors had to decorate the sitting room and the dining room with the traditional kinds of paper chains and other Christmassy features. Emma's Christmas cards populated the mantelpiece and hung on bright red ribbons down the side of the fireplace. A Christmas tree was planned, but Emma wanted to get that done with her visitors as part of the build up to the Christmas festivities.

Sara noticed how even Peter joined in with hanging the decorations, and seemed to enjoy himself. The Calderwood-Morrises were less enthusiastic, but they helped, and Roland was soon organizing everyone with what they should be doing. Sara wondered why he and his wife hadn't gone abroad somewhere, because neither seemed very interested in Christmas traditions. On the other hand, Sara reasoned that they'd perhaps been travelling abroad so long they'd lost touch and needed to get back into the swing of it all again.

Sometimes, when Sara and Peter were talking about local attractions or Christmas, Sara caught a glimpse of wistfulness in Veronica's eyes, though she rarely joined the conversation unless someone asked her something directly. Sara felt sorry for her. Perhaps Veronica lived her life through Roland, and had forgotten to live it her own way.

The next morning, when she looked out of the window, the sky was slate-grey and filled with dark stormy clouds. Rain hit the window diagonally. Sara resigned herself to a morning with her paperback. That was no punishment, because most of her time recently had been spent on making Katie's costume. The weather cleared during the course of the day, and by lunchtime the wind was merely stirring gently amongst the branches of the trees, and the sun was trying bravely to make up for lost time.

* * *

Alex was punctual and Sara was waiting. She hurried out when she saw him draw up outside. He leaned forward from his driving seat and opened the door. She slid into the passenger seat and smiled her thanks.

'Are you ready for the performance of the century?' she asked him.

His eyes twinkled. 'As ready as I'll ever be. If Katie doesn't soon get the chance to show off her costume, she'll be impossible to live with. I've listened to the handful of words she has to speak at least a thousand times.'

Sara settled into her seat. 'Ah, but that's not the same as standing in front of a live audience. Has she ever done anything like this before?'

Alex started the car and checked the mirror before he pulled out onto the road. 'No, so I don't know how she'll react. My mother- and father-in-law wanted to come, but she has a long-awaited appointment about a hip replacement this afternoon and he's going with her. They're very disappointed.' He shrugged.

'Can't be helped. My parents are also away on holiday and won't be back until tomorrow.'

'Why don't you film it with your phone? I have mine with me, although I'm not sure if the battery still has enough power.'

'That's a good idea.' He sounded almost relieved. 'I hadn't thought of that. They'll be pleased, and Katie can see herself on the stage.'

Minutes later they arrived. Cars were parked all along the approach road, and Alex managed to tuck his into a convenient spot not too far away. The small school was red-brick, its windows decorated with Christmas motifs and strings of cotton-wool snowballs. They followed a group of other people through the entrance door and into the largest room in the building. Sara noticed someone nodding occasionally to Alex, and he responded. They eyed her with puzzlement. In a small place like this, if Alex turned up with a strange woman at his side, Sara could imagine some busy tongues would get even busier until Emma put them in the picture.

There was a buzz of conversation and the sound of laughter tinged with heightened excitement. Alex was tall, and his confident movement soon got them through the muddle to some seats on the edge of the row, not far from the stage.

Sara felt transported back to her own schooldays. She looked at the simple curtains hiding the platform, at a piano tucked away in a nearby corner, and at the windows covered in stars and edged with silver. She spotted Emma at the back of the room, busy arranging several plates of mince pies and dozens of teacups on a trestle table. Emma saw her too, smiled and waved.

There were a lot of comings and goings. A young woman hurrying down the aisle stopped when she saw Alex. She eyed Sara and couldn't hide the surprise in her face. 'Hello, Alex! Glad you could make it. Katie's very excited but I'm sure she'll be okay.'

He nodded. 'Let's hope so.' He looked at Sara briefly and then explained politely, 'This is Sara. She's staying with Emma, and she made Katie's costume. Sara, this is Megan Butler. She's Katie's teacher.'

Sara smiled. 'Hello!'

Megan Butler was young, very attractive, and slim, with curly brown hair and hazel eyes. She declared, 'That was very kind of you, especially as you're a visitor. It's excellent, one of the best costumes.'

'I was pleased to help. I enjoyed doing it, apart from peeling the bits of glue off my fingers every night.'

'Unfortunately I couldn't offer to help Katie, although I would have liked to. I knew it would be difficult for you, Alex, but I couldn't single Katie out. The other parents would have been up in arms! I presumed Emma would help you.' She gave Alex a smile and explained, 'Alex and I are good friends. We've known each other since kindergarten.' She looked at her watch briefly and waved some papers in her hand. 'Must rush and get things going. See you later, Alex.'

Soon after, Megan Butler stood centre stage, and quiet descended on the room. She welcomed everyone and announced who was playing each part. She was confident and clearly used to being in charge. When she left the stage, she went towards the piano, sat down and played 'Silent Night' to set the atmosphere. The curtains opened and the play began.

It went well, even if the little girl playing Mary forgot some of her words in her nervousness and had to be prompted. Katie didn't forget a single one of hers, and she really looked like a little angel. The costume and her blonde hair and blue eyes completed the angelic impression she was meant to make.

Sara had a lump in her throat and didn't dare think about looking across at Alex, not for a moment. She knew he was filming it all with his phone, but she had no doubt that thoughts about his dead wife were whizzing through his brain at a moment like this. She wondered if that would ever end. Probably not. Katie was part of him, and part of her mother. The little girl didn't look like him, so it was likely she resembled her mother. As she grew older, each and every event was likely to remind Alex of Katie's mother.

When the curtains closed, clapping thundered throughout the room, and various parents and grandparents hooted and whistled their approval. The children reappeared on stage to bow and smile. Most of them had bright red cheeks from the excitement, and each one of them began searching the audience for the person or persons they wanted to impress most of all.

The clapping faded and parents hurried forward to claim their children. Alex went to lift Katie down off the stage. He whispered in her ear and she beamed from one side of her face to the other. They joined Sara, waiting where he'd left her.

'You were great, Katie,' Sara said. 'One of the best angels I've ever seen. You didn't forget a single word!'

Katie nodded. In her high-pitched voice, she said, 'And you helped to make my costume. The others thought it was super.'

Alex looked at her. 'Yes, we have to thank Sara. I'm sure you would've turned up looking like a white sack with droopy wings that kept falling off if she hadn't helped us.'

Megan Butler rushed over. 'Well done, Katie! You were all good, but this year's angel made a great impression.'

Like sunshine emerging after a spell of rain, Katie looked at her teacher and smiled.

Megan asked him, 'I hope you're staying for mince pies and a cup of tea?'

'Well, I wasn't planning to, but it might give Katie a few minutes to calm down.'

She nodded. 'I'll see you later. I have

to mingle with all the parents, otherwise they'll complain.' She turned and hurried off into the throng.

Still holding Katie in his arms, which was difficult because of the wings, he and Sara made their way to where Emma was standing with a broad smile and a teapot in her hand.

6

Sara slipped away after standing to the side with a cup of tea and a mince pie for a couple of minutes. Other people descended on Alex and kept him busy talking, then someone dragged him away and he was soon lost in the crowd. Sara had the feeling that because they'd seen her come with Alex, her presence was puzzling them, but they didn't like to ask who she was or what she was doing there.

She told Emma she was going. The roads were empty, and a full moon lit up the hedges along the way. Pools of shadows scrambled along the verges, and her breath froze on the night air. She felt happy and rather silly as she went along, deliberately blowing bursts of chilled air in front of her like a child. Everything was very silent and special. Christmas was approaching fast, and somehow the atmosphere was stronger here than in town. Perhaps it was because everyone knew each other. She missed the fun of being with her family, but she was enjoying herself in a way she never expected.

Back at Emma's, the house was lit up and Sara could see the decorations through the windows. She walked briskly up the path and went straight upstairs. After taking her things off, she threw herself onto the bed and looked up at the ceiling. She crossed her hands behind her head and thought how lucky she was. She had a good job and some nice friends, she was healthy, she'd avoided the disaster of a wrong man, and she had a loving family. What more could anyone want?

She heard Emma returning and went back downstairs. Removing her coat, Emma said, 'I left them to it. It's time to get the evening meal. I prepared it this morning, so I only have to heat it up and make a salad.'

'Need any help?'

Emma shook her head. 'Thanks, but I can manage. Sometimes I forget you're a visitor because you seem to fit in so easily, as if you've always been here. Go into the sitting room now and join the others. Tell them food will be on the table in half an hour.'

There were voices in the sitting room. Sara discovered one belonged to Roland Calderwood-Morris. He was standing in front of the fire, his hands crossed behind his back with the kind of military bearing that said it all. Veronica looked up and smiled when Sara arrived.

Sara decided to be social. 'I've just been to see the local school's play. It was fun. Small children can be real devils, but put them in a costume and they're transformed.'

Veronica said, 'Yes, great fun I'm sure. The costume you made for the little girl was lovely. I expect she stole the show?'

'Well I'm not sure about that. All the mothers did their best. It's not always easy to live up to expectations. I bet that a lot of parents have never made a costume of any kind before and have no idea how to set about it.'

Roland shifted his position and joined in. 'I suppose you have to have plenty of creativity for that sort of thing.'

'A lot of my work is computerized these days, but I still need lots of imagination to come up with the right idea. We have to produce what the customer wants and needs, and sometimes they're not even sure themselves what they want.'

'Is yours a big company?'

'No. We're only twenty people, but the company has a good reputation. I'm thinking of looking for something new. I'm even toying with looking for a job abroad for a while.' Sara had already decided she'd avoid working with Paul anymore, if she could.

Roland brushed the edge of his moustache upward, and looked happier to talk about familiar ground. 'That's the way, my dear. Go and experience other countries and cultures. Veronica and I have seen a bit of the world, and it hasn't done us any harm, has it old girl? Even if we were always glad to come back to old Blighty.'

'Are you still in active service?'

'No, left a short while ago. We're still deciding where to put down our roots. Looking for a place where we can be useful in the community. I'd like to join the boards of things like the golf club, the British Legion and such. I'm good at organizing, and I think my experience would be useful for that sort of thing.'

Sara wondered if his good intentions would be thwarted. He was likely to bulldoze any opposition, and tended to think his ideas were the only option. An army title didn't carry the weight it once did, although she admitted that his organizing skills might help a struggling group who couldn't find any volunteers to do the donkeywork. 'Are you looking forward to settling down,

Veronica?' she asked.

She looked almost as if she hadn't given it much thought. After a second or two, she said, 'Yes, I think it'll be nice to have our own things around us after so many years of living in army quarters. It'll be good to know we've settled somewhere at last.'

Emma tucked her head round the door. 'Spare a minute, Sara?'

'Yes, of course.' She got up and followed her out. To her surprise, Alex was in the hall.

'You disappeared before we could bring you back,' he said. 'I wanted to repeat how grateful I am for your help.'

Colour crept up her cheeks. She felt like a giddy teenager. 'You've said that a couple of times already, and I honestly enjoyed helping. Katie was a star. Where is she?'

'Still in the car. I think she's tired out. It was all the excitement, I expect. It's not worth bringing her in. I'm not stopping.' His gaze travelled her face and he paused before he said, 'You should've waited.'

'I didn't want to cause any more gossip.' He looked puzzled so she explained, 'I had a feeling that because I came with you, people were speculating about why I was there. It wasn't far to walk. Only a couple of minutes.'

He met her glance. 'Oh! I see. I didn't notice . . . but then, I'm used to it. Trying to match me up is a favourite pastime with some people.'

'And it doesn't annoy you?'

'A bit, but I try to ignore it as best I can.'

'But doesn't it make it difficult for you to have a private life?'

He met her glance. 'I assure you, I'd never let village gossip rule my life.' He stuck his hands into his pockets and seemed resolved. 'Katie jogged my senses and suggested it'd be nice to invite you to tea on Sunday, to say thank you. I thought it was an excellent idea.'

Sara was startled. Her heartbeat

quickened noticeably and she tried to hide her surprise. 'That's very kind of you and Katie. But only if you don't go to any special trouble.'

He laughed softly. 'A shop-bought cake and Katie's cucumber sandwiches, is that okay?'

'And the gossip?'

'Forget it. You're a visitor. If you feel happier, I'll invite Katie's grandparents to be chaperones. They'll be delighted to see Katie in the play — as soon as I figure out how to get it from my phone onto the TV.'

If his parents-in-law were there, the situation would be harmless. But why should she worry? Alex was an attractive widower who was coping with his life very well on his own. He wasn't looking for an affair, or any other kind of relationship. 'Send it as an email attachment to your computer,' she told him. 'Download it and then burn it onto a DVD.' He nodded.

Peter came clattering down the narrow stairs and saw them. He paused.

'Hi, Sara. Had a good day? How did the play go?'

'Very well. Katie was a real star. Peter, this is Alex Crossley, Katie's father.' For Alex's benefit, she added, 'And this is Peter Terrell, a fellow visitor. Peter helped me to glue on dozens and dozens of the feathers, so you see it wasn't all my work.'

The two men sized each other up and nodded. Sara noticed that Alex didn't extend the invitation to include Peter.

'Well, I must be off; Katie's waiting. See you on Sunday, then? About three would be fine.'

Sara nodded. 'Till Sunday.' He turned on his heel and left.

Peter queried, 'An invitation?'

'He feels obliged to invite me as thanks for making Katie's costume. His parents-in-law will be there too.' Sara didn't know why she added that. She didn't need to justify herself to anyone.

Peter nodded and opened the door to the sitting room for them to join the others.

* * *

For some reason, Sara felt nervous when she walked to Alex's home on Sunday afternoon. Like every morning recently, there was a sprinkling of frost, and she'd even seen a weak snow shower just before breakfast. It didn't stick, and by now there was no sign of it anymore. She looked up at grey clouds and wondered if they really would get a white Christmas this year. She was limited in her choice of what to wear; she hadn't reckoned with invitations to afternoon tea. In the end she chose a long grey skirt, a fashionable sweater in a flattering shade of purplish-blue, and her best soft leather boots.

When she reached Alex's driveway, there was an unknown car standing in front of the garage. She wondered why her pulse accelerated when she thought about seeing Alex again. She was used to customers and strangers; she'd never felt this edgy before. She rang the bell and heard Katie's excited voice, followed by steps coming to the door. When it opened, Sara felt almost breathless for a moment as she met Alex's eyes, then smiled and hid her confusion by bending to give Katie a puzzle she'd bought last time she was in town.

'Hi, Katie,' she said. 'I thought you'd like this. It's a picture of farmhouse animals. I think you'll manage it on your own. It says it's for five- to seven-year-olds, so it's your age range.'

Katie nodded, her eyes sparkling as she clutched the gift to her chest. She wore a pink and white dress, pink tights, and pink ribbons in her hair. 'Thank you,' she said, then danced off again.

'That was thoughtful,' Alex said warmly, 'but completely unnecessary with Christmas just around the corner. She gets too much already. Come in and let me take your coat. The living room is straight on.'

Sara followed Katie and found

herself in a large room that overlooked the garden at the rear. There wasn't much colour there at this time of year, but the lawn was edged with bushes and flowerbeds, and there was an attractive copse of trees with an inviting bench in one of the corners. She turned her attention to two people sitting in some soft leather armchairs.

Sara smiled but didn't need to introduce herself, as Katie did it for her. 'This is Sara. She helped me make my costume.'

The man, middle-aged with salt-and-pepper hair and a kind face, smiled and got up to shake hands. 'Hello, Sara. We're pleased to meet you. Katie told us all about how you turned her into a first-class angel. I'm Nigel Barlow, and this is my wife Penny.'

Sara shook his hand. 'Hello! Nice to meet you.' She shook hands with Penny, who eyed her more carefully, but not unkindly. She was comfortably round with blue eyes and carefully arranged blonde hair.

Alex joined them, and gestured to the cream couch where Katie had already made herself comfortable and was already looking at the cover of the puzzle. 'Sit down. Tea won't be long. Penny brought a cake with her, so I can offer you something that's home-baked after all. I'll just make the tea. Katie, will you come and help with the sandwiches and plates, please?' She hopped down and trotted after him towards the kitchen.

'Alex explained you're a visitor and staying over Christmas with Emma Arber?' Nigel said to Sara.

'Yes.' She explained about her parent's silver-wedding present.

'And you don't mind — I mean, celebrating among strangers?'

'No. I thought I'd be spending my time tucked away in my room reading, but the whole week has flown. I spent one afternoon helping Emma to decorate the church, went for a long walk with one of the other visitors another day, helped Katie with her costume, and then watched the play on Friday.'

Penny said, 'I'm awfully grateful you did the costume. I find I'm all fingers and thumbs this week. It would've been a big challenge for me.' She smiled and added, 'I'm not usually so nervous, but . . . '

Sara gave her a sympathetic smile. 'Don't give it a second thought. Alex mentioned you had an appointment about a hip replacement on Friday? How did it go?'

Penny's forehead wrinkled. 'The specialist gave me a date, a month after Christmas.'

'And are you worried?'

'A little,' she admitted. 'It all sounds quite complicated.'

'I don't think anyone looks forward to an operation, but I think hip replacements are fairly routine these days. My neighbour had one at the beginning of this year. It turned out really well. She had to use crutches for six weeks after the operation, but she said that was because she had to keep the weight off her hip to give it a chance to heal, rather than because she wasn't able to walk properly. She went for physiotherapy for a while and that helped a lot. Nowadays you'd never know she has an artificial joint. She was absolutely delighted to be free of pain for the first time in years. Are you in pain?'

'Yes, that's why I finally gave in and decided I had to do something. Some days I can only get through with the help of painkillers, but I don't want to rely on them forevermore. I've been on the waiting list for ages, and I'll be glad to get it over and done with now.'

'If you'd like to talk to someone who's gone through the same thing, I'll give you her telephone number. I know that Mimi's surgeon asked if she'd help to reassure a couple of his patients. She did. She's a lovely person.'

Alex came in with a tray loaded with tea things, sandwiches and an iced fruitcake. He distributed crockery and told them all to help themselves before he made himself comfortable in one of the other chairs.

Katie piped in, 'I made the sandwiches with Dad. He sliced the cucumber because he wouldn't let me use the knife, but I did the rest on my own.'

'And they look very tempting, my love,' Nigel pronounced.

They all did justice to Katie's efforts and Penny's baking skills. Topics of conversation meandered through local and national news, and the coming Christmas festivities. Sara noted the festoon of colourful paper chains trimming the walls and the artificial Christmas tree in the window. Alex was doing his best.

His parents-in-law asked about where she came from, her family and her job. She mused that it must be hard for them to come to terms with new developments in Alex's life. Alex seemed to have kept up a good relationship with them, and that was good. The DVD and the TV were all set up and they watched the nativity play again.

Katie's grandparents were enchanted. Sara could see the pride and delight in their faces and Katie looked in wonder when she saw herself on stage. If Alex ever remarried, she hoped his ex-parents-in-law would be magnanimous enough to realize that it was better for him to share his life with someone else again, and give Katie the chance to grow up in a proper family. Sara shook herself free of her wanderings. What did it matter whether his parents-in-law could adjust or not? It had nothing to do with her. She'd be leaving after Christmas.

Everyone agreed that Katie was a star. Sara asked, 'What's happening to the costume?'

He laughed. 'It's hanging on the wardrobe door. I expect someone else will be delighted to get it next year.'

Sounding quite determined, Katie insisted, 'No, Daddy! I'm going to keep it forever and ever.'

116

Soon afterwards, after another cup of tea, the Barlows began to gather their things together, and Nigel helped his wife to her feet. She leaned heavily on his arm when she walked. Sara followed them into the hall.

It was her opening to leave too. She said, 'Thank you for the tea. The sandwiches were really delicious.'

Katie smiled smugly. Nigel and Penny said goodbye to her politely.

Sara said, 'Good luck with the operation, Penny.'

The older woman smiled. 'I've been thinking — I'd like your neighbour's telephone number if you don't mind. It would help to talk to someone else who's gone through it all.'

Sara ruffled through her shoulder bag and found Mimi's address and telephone number. She scribbled them on the back of a scrap of paper. 'Just phone and explain. I'm sure she'll try to reassure you.'

Katie hugged and kissed her grandparents and stood with Alex watching them leave. Nigel helped his wife into the passenger seat. By then Sara had slipped into her coat, and joined Alex and Katie to wave them off.

Alex looked down at his daughter. 'Let's get some fresh air, Katie. We'll walk Sara back to Emma's.'

Sara was slightly flustered. He didn't seem the kind of man who'd intentionally prolong visiting time with a passing acquaintance. There was no reason for her to refuse their company, so she waited until they'd donned their scarves and coats, and they set off together. Emma's home was just a couple of minutes away.

Sara felt a little tongue-tied at first, but Katie chattered about the play and Alex pointed out some distant landmarks as they went. Katie was soon skipping along far ahead of them.

'She'll stay on the pavement, I hope?'

'Yes. I've warned her that if she doesn't, she'll have to hold someone's hand all the time, and of course she's much too big for that now!'

Sara laughed softly. Stuffing her gloved hands deeper into her pockets, she said, 'I like the village. It's very self-contained and traditional, but good.'

'Yes, I know what you mean. It can be suffocating though. When my wife died, it wasn't possible to put my head outside the door for months afterwards without getting another shower of sympathetic and pitying words. Once I'd adapted a bit, I didn't mind quite so much.'

'I'm sorry — I mean about your wife. I can imagine it was a very difficult time for you and the people who knew you both. Probably no one knew how to react. They couldn't pretend they didn't care, and thought the only thing they could do was to give you positive support and encouragement by talking about it all the time.'

He stopped, and she had to stop as well and face him. 'You're very perceptive. Yes, I realized that later.' He looked over a nearby hedge into the distance. 'Susan and I grew up together. She was a special person, gentle and sweet. She didn't deserve to die, or to worry until the last second about Katie. That was her biggest concern. She knew how much I love Katie and that I'd always protect her, but how can you reassure the mother of a two-year-old little girl she has to leave behind that she'll be cared for in the same way as she would have done herself?'

Sara felt tears at the back of her eyes. 'You can't. Does Katie remember her?'

'Only from photos now. At the time Katie did ask for her a lot, but it's natural that the memories soon blurred. I try to keep them alive by repeating things and showing her photos, because every little girl needs to know she has a mother.'

'You're doing a great job. From what I hear from Emma, you've reorganized your life around her needs; and Katie's a happy, cheerful little girl. I'm sure your wife would've been very proud of how you've managed.'

He ran his hand down his face. 'It's getting easier. She's growing more independent with every passing year, and I've found I can handle a little schoolgirl better than a toddler in nappies.'

Sara laughed. 'I bet.' They continued on their way, and Sara felt how the cold air had brought the colour to her cheeks. 'Your wife's parents are very nice.'

'Yes. They helped me a lot when it happened, even though they were fighting their own demons. Time does blunt the pain and has helped us all to get through the mess. My parents have a smallholding a couple of miles away, and everyone took turns to look after Katie if I was away on business. Emma was always prepared to help too, but then Emma is always helping someone, somewhere.'

'Yes, Emma's so involved with everything. I'm amazed she has time to take in visitors.'

Alex shrugged. 'She doesn't have much of a pension. She needs the extra money. That son of hers prefers to spend his money on trips abroad or the newest model of a favoured car. Emma defends him like a dragon, but I find him wanting. We don't like each other much.'

'I met him recently. He called to see Emma. I got the impression he was a smooth operator, but he seems to be doing well in his job — otherwise he wouldn't have so much money, would he?'

'I suppose not, but that doesn't make him more amiable in my eyes. He's a couple of years younger than me and used to hang out with a shady lot at school. I hope for Emma's sake that he's left that all behind him.'

They'd reached Emma's. The door was open. Katie ran inside to look for Emma. When they reached the door, Alex said, 'Send Katie out, Sara. Tell Emma I'll see her tomorrow as usual. I want to go over some figures before a meeting tomorrow, so I don't have time to stop and chat now.'

She nodded and turned to go. To her surprise, he leaned forward and kissed her on the cheek. Colour flooded her face as she looked at him. He added, 'Thanks for everything, and for being a good listener.'

Confused, she managed to utter, 'There's nothing to thank me for. I enjoyed the tea and our walk back. I'll tell Katie you're waiting.' She turned away quickly, hoping she could hide the turmoil and uncertainty in her face from him and not show what his gesture had roused in her. It wasn't just his interest and the knowledge that he accepted her that caused her heartbeat to quicken, and it wasn't because he was attractive to look at either. It was something to do with what she already knew about him, and the feeling about all that she could still learn if she wanted to. Sara warned herself not to mistake sympathy for anything else. They were ships passing in the night, and Alex Crossley was much too complicated for someone who had just dumped her boyfriend and wasn't looking for a replacement.

7

The next morning, still confused and thinking about Alex's innocent kiss, Sara decided that a long walk in the fresh air would help. She didn't have enough courage to walk Peter's moorland route, as she might get lost, so she chose to follow the road into town. Peter had already left on one of his tours before she came down for breakfast. She went into the sitting room to look for a tourist map of the area to stick in her pocket, just in case she wasn't sure where she was. She found Veronica looking listlessly out of the window.

'What are you planning to do today?' Sara asked her.

Veronica looked up. She looked startled and surprised. 'Roland has gone to find out about organizations and prospects locally. I pleaded a headache and decided to stay put.'

Sara laughed. 'Well I can understand why. It sounds like a lot of driving around looking for people who aren't available. I'm going to walk into town. I don't really need anything, but I decided some fresh air would do me good.' She paused. 'I could go by car, but it won't take longer than an hour to walk there. I don't suppose you'd like to come, would you? I intend to be back long before teatime.'

Veronica brightened noticeably. She probably didn't get many invitations or opportunities to do something without Roland. 'Yes, I'd like that.'

'Wrap up, then. It's a decent walk, and I imagine it's pretty cold out there this morning.'

'I don't mind. I'm used to the cold. We've been stationed in some wild places, and some of them were pretty cold.'

'That sounds interesting. You can tell me about them as we go along.'

A short time later they were on

their way. Veronica was used to keeping up with her husband's long strides, so she had no trouble walking alongside Sara. She chattered about some of the places they'd been and had a stimulating way of describing them. Sara asked appropriate questions, and Veronica asked Sara about her lifestyle. Sara mused that although Veronica had given her an initial impression that she was a grey mouse, she wasn't. She'd experienced places and happenings that few other women had. She'd travelled, been in some outlandish locations, and gained knowledge about other cultures and people. They both settled down to each other's company.

'What did you do before you got married?' Sara asked.

'I was a chief librarian in London.'

'Really? Then you must have very good qualifications.'

She said casually, 'I studied English Literature and History at Cambridge, and then did my training as a librarian.

I always wanted to do something with books.'

'Gosh! And you gave all that up after you got married. Why?'

'Roland was a very dashing figure when we met, and there was no need for me to work after we married. I enjoyed being cared for.' They were fighting the wind on a particular open stretch of the road and were both glad to turn the corner into a quieter section. Veronica continued, 'I hoped we'd have children, but it didn't happen. New quarters in new surroundings, and meeting new people, wasn't something that I enjoyed much. Sometimes we were in cities; sometimes we were out in the wilderness. If I ever started to think about finding some kind of work, usually Roland got a new posting. In the end I ignored the possibility of doing something.'

'What a shame. What a waste of your qualifications and experience. Didn't you get bored? Or was it a continuous round of champagne breakfasts and tennis tournaments among the military wives?'

Veronica giggled. 'That's what people think about army wives, but it's not like that, believe me. Even if it was, I'm not the type to get involved in that kind of hen party. Mostly our postings were pretty mundane, and I just accepted the good with the bad. Roland had a responsible job and was always busy. I didn't want to add to his problems unless it couldn't be helped. I tried to keep myself busy as best I could.'

'Even if you were moving around all the time, you could've done something worthwhile, with your qualifications. What about teaching? You might've enjoyed that.'

She laughed. 'Perhaps, but in a lot of the places the children didn't get any kind of schooling because their parents couldn't afford to send them, or they were needed to work alongside their parents in the fields. I doubt if learning English was high on their lists of essentials. I often helped with charity work, and Roland encouraged that. He didn't expect more of me than a tidy house, a tasty meal, and domestic tranquillity.'

Sara was slightly dazed. 'But what about you? What about what you wanted? If you were childless, Roland must have realized you had too much spare time on your hands.'

Veronica nodded and pulled her woollen hat tighter round her head. 'Especially in places where we were expected to employ someone local to do the housework and the garden. It felt unreal sometimes, and I missed having something useful to do. I started to write a book once, when we were in a desolate region, and when Roland was out most of the day or even away for a day or two. It was a historical novel and an enjoyable pastime. Luckily most of the places soldiers are stationed these days have access to the internet, and I had my laptop, so I was able to research quite easily if I wasn't sure about details.'

'What was it about?'

'One of the lesser-known Plantagenets.'

'And what happened to the book?'

'I finished it, and it's still in the bottom of my suitcase.'

'You didn't try to find a publisher?'

'No. I liked writing it, but I'm not vain enough to think it's good enough to be published.'

Sara's eyes widened. 'I'll be damned! You should at least try. Know what? We're going to buy a big padded envelope in town and look up names of suitable publishers in the local library.'

Veronica looked flustered. 'But it may be complete rubbish. No one has ever read it.'

'With your knowledge of history, I think you have as good a chance as anyone else to produce a decent book. Does Roland know that you finished it?'

'He used to tease me about it and call it my 'scribblings'. I don't think he took it seriously.'

'Well he should have.'

Veronica smiled and looked almost young. 'Roland isn't as bossy and overbearing as he seems. I know he gives strangers that impression, but he's always looked after me and protected me ever since we married, and he's never been unfaithful like so many other diplomats and officers I've met. He may seem pompous, but he's still the reliable, decent, caring man I fell in love with. I was over thirty when we met. I had no family; my parents were already dead. I tended to bury myself in my work, and then suddenly this smart officer turned up in the library one day looking for specialist information. I still thank heaven he did.' She took her hanky out of her pocket and blew her nose. 'I don't know why I'm telling you all this. I've never met anyone quite like you before.'

Sara chuckled. 'We are going to get those envelopes and find some addresses. You can surprise Roland this evening by telling him you're sending your manuscript to a publisher. It'll be interesting to see how he reacts.'

Sara was glad Veronica had come with her. Not only had she found out that Veronica wasn't such a grey mouse after all, but the older woman had also presented Roland in a kinder light. His bluff and hearty attitude to the world in general hid the fact that he seemed to care a lot for Veronica, and she for him. More than anyone could suppose at first glance.

They reached the town, did their shopping and found all they wanted. They then settled next to a corner table in one of the cafés to enjoy some fragrant coffee and a delicious pastry. They were just about to leave for home when Veronica remembered she'd have to make a printed copy before she could send it anywhere. She'd lugged her present copy around in the bottom of her suitcase for some time, and it was now dog-eared and shabby. She had the story stored on her laptop, but she'd need paper, and she needed a fresh copy. They found paper quite easily at the stationer's, but they couldn't find a copy shop. That meant Veronica would have to persuade Roland to make a trip to the next biggest town.

* * *

The next morning, Sara was anxious to hear how Roland had reacted. A glance out of the window told her it was still very cold, and once again a white sprinkling of frost covered everything. Coming down stairs, she met Emma with a coffee pot.

'Morning, Emma!' Emma looked anxious and worried. 'Is something wrong?'

Emma nodded. 'Paul just rang with some bad news. Someone's stolen some old pictures from the church. Paul is upset and feels very guilty, because Janet's husband has been trying to persuade him to lock the church up at night for ages, and now this has happened.'

'Oh dear, how awful. Janet mentioned that the church was at risk. I can't remember seeing any paintings. Where were they? Are they valuable?'

'They aren't paintings, and perhaps the word 'pictures' is also misleading. 'Wooden carvings' would be a better description. They hung on the wall on the far side of the altar. They aren't very big, and they've darkened a lot with age, so I don't suppose many people would notice them straight off. There are — there were — three of them depicting the life of Christ. His birth, his life, and his crucifixion.'

'And I presume that they're old? And valuable?'

Emma was flustered. 'I'm not sure. We didn't have much time to talk about details. They've always been in the church as far as I know, and I presume they're valuable in their own way. I don't even know if Paul has ever thought about what they might be worth. Who'd steal from a church? How can anybody do such a thing?'

Sara shrugged. 'That's how it is these days. Nothing is sacred.' She put her hand over her mouth. 'Sorry, I wasn't trying to be funny. It just slipped out. I suppose Paul has called Janet's husband?'

Emma nodded. 'He's informed the county constabulary and they're arranging for detectives to come and check and talk to Paul about it. We don't even know if anyone has ever taken any pictures of them. Paul's hoping someone in the historical society has; he was on his way round to talk to Ben Harker to find out. Come on, have your breakfast. Have you planned anything special for this morning?'

Sara followed her into the dining room. 'No. If I can help you or Paul in any way, just say so.'

Peter was up and gone. Veronica and Roland weren't down yet, so Sara had a peaceful breakfast. After she'd glanced through the newspaper, she wondered if Veronica would persuade Roland to take her to the copy shop in the next big town. If not, she'd offer to go for her. She took her breakfast things back to the kitchen and told Emma about Veronica's book and how it needed to be printed out again before she could send it off.

Emma nodded. 'How nice, and how clever. She's a very quiet person, but behind the stiff facade she's very pleasant. She's probably got into the habit of being cautious about making friends, if they were always on the move.' She paused. 'I was just thinking — you need a printer? What about asking Alex? I know he's got one at home, and he probably has more than one in his office.'

Sara was flustered. 'Oh, I wouldn't want to bother him.'

'Don't be silly. You helped him with Katie's costume. I bet he'll be glad to help you. Paul has a printer, but he'll be busy this morning with this police business. He's already left the vicarage, and I don't know when I'll be able to grab him to ask for help now. I'll phone Alex and ask him instead.'

Sara opened her mouth to protest, but Emma was already on the way to the hall. She felt butterflies rising in her stomach as she thought about Alex. She couldn't help herself fantasizing about him, although she tried hard. If she got too interested, it would only make the situation more confusing.

A few minutes later, Emma returned and smiled. 'No problem. He says you can come to his office any time. I'll give you his address. It's easy to find. It's down a side street in the next village — not the one you went to yesterday. You have to go in the other direction.'

★   ★   ★

When The Calderwood-Morrises came down, Sara waited in the sitting room until they'd finished breakfast. When they entered the living room, she could tell from Veronica's lively expression

138

that she'd told her husband about her book.

After the usual generalities, Sara said, 'Did Veronica tell you how I said she should submit her book to a publisher?'

'Yes, and you're right of course. I must admit, I'd forgotten all about it because she never talked about it much, even at the time. I know she's got a clever brain, and I'm sure she's got what it takes to produce an entertaining read. I agree with you — she should try to find a publisher. If I'd known it was finished, I'd have encouraged her long ago.'

'Good, because I've just arranged to get it printed. Alex has a printer at his office and he's offered to help. It'll save you a trip to a copy shop in town. When I told Emma and explained that Veronica needed a printed copy, she phoned Alex. I think I've got a spare memory stick among my things, if you haven't got one. Once you copy the book onto that, I'll drive over to Alex's office and ask him to do the rest.'

Roland brushed his moustache. 'I must say, it's jolly decent of everyone. It should be my job to sort it all out, but as you know Alex and he says it isn't too much bother, we'll be grateful. Fighting our way through the mass of Christmas shoppers today wasn't a welcome prospect.' He threw his arm around his wife's shoulder.

Veronica's cheeks were bright pink and her eyes sparkled. She looked across at Sara. 'I think I have a stick myself. If not, I'll come back.' She slipped out of her husband's embrace and hurried out of the room.

Roland followed her with his eyes and said, 'She deserves a break. I hope the book is successful, and I wish I'd remembered how much time she spent writing it. I bet she's produced a spanking good story. I never met any other army wife in the course of my whole career who accepted so many changes and new situations without grumbling like she has. She's always been an utter brick!'

Sara nodded, and a few minutes later Veronica came back and handed her the memory stick with the story. Breathlessly she explained that they were going to the village for stamps, and taking the old manuscript along with them to find how much it would cost to send it. Once they had the fresh copy, they'd just need to put the stamps on the envelope and send it off. Sara promised to be back in time for Veronica to get it ready for the day's last collection.

It was still early. After leaving Roland and Veronica, she went to the kitchen to ask Emma for directions to Alex's office, and then back upstairs to check her make-up. Then she told herself she was being silly. Why would Alex notice whether she was wearing lipstick or not?

8

Sara found his office easily. It was a square functional building with lots of floor-length windows situated on the edge of a small industrial estate. When she walked in, she discovered herself directly in the main office where a handful of people were working at their desks or in front of computers.

Alex had a small room, with an opaque lower section of glass, in one of the corners. He was standing with some papers in his hands and telephoning when he saw Sara. He looked up, waved and beckoned her across. Some other men, busy at their desks, looked up with interest too, and responded politely when she said 'Good morning!' on her way. The only woman in the room was behind a desk near Alex's cubbyhole. She had a friendly face and gave Sara a smile.

'Go straight in,' she said. 'Alex is expecting you.'

Sara noticed that he looked very relaxed in jeans and a checked shirt with an open collar. Its sleeves were rolled up to his elbows. 'Hi!' he greeted her.

She felt nervous but managed a return smile. 'Hi, Alex. Thanks for coming to the rescue.'

'What's it about? Emma said you needed to print a book. What book? Have you written one?'

She laughed. 'No; I wish I had enough talent. Veronica has.' She noted his puzzled expression. 'Veronica's one of the other visitors. She's married to the ex-army officer, Roland. She wrote this book when he was off having military adventures and she was stuck somewhere on her own, with nothing to do. It's a historical novel. I've persuaded her to send it to a publisher, so she needs a printed copy.'

His dark eyes twinkled. 'You think she has talent? There are probably millions of would-be authors waiting for a chance.'

Sara liked his relaxed attitude. 'I don't know if it's good or not; I haven't read it. But I do know she studied History at Cambridge, and it's a historical novel about one of the Plantagenets, so I think she might have a better chance of succeeding than a lot of other people who haven't got her background knowledge. Anyway, I want to boost her confidence, since she seems to have always hidden her talents under a bushel. She deserves a chance.'

Alex considered her quietly for a moment. 'She's lucky to have met you. Not many people would bother. You seem to have an inborn tendency to be helpful, don't you?'

She coloured. 'It just looks like that. But I'm on holiday, and I have the time. I wouldn't be able to bother about something like this if I was at work.'

He nodded and said, 'Give me the stick. I'll get Pam to print it out for you. How many pages are there?'

'Roughly four hundred, I think.' She handed him the memory stick and ruffled through her capacious bag for the pack of paper. 'Here's some paper, and Veronica told me she'd like to pay you the printing costs.'

'I wouldn't do it for just anyone, but since you're asking . . . And of course I'm reckoning that she'll mention us in her acknowledgements if it turns out to be a bestseller.'

He went out into the main office, and Sara could see him handing things to Pam, the lady who had greeted her. She smiled at him and nodded before she got up and went off to another section divided off from the rest of the room. Sara presumed the printers were isolated to reduce their noise.

On his way back, one of the men called to Alex. He leaned over the man's desk to look at the computer and his jeans hugged his hips in a very pleasing way. Sara admitted he was young enough, and attractive enough, to waken dormant thoughts in her

145

brain. She reminded herself quickly that he was a widower and not interested in changing that status.

The two men had a short conversation; the man pointed at the screen and after a brief discussion Alex nodded. He came back and said to Sara, 'Sorry about that. Gary wanted to make sure I was in agreement with his suggestions. Luckily our printers take USB sticks, so we won't have to transfer back and forth between the computer and the printer. It shouldn't take long. Sit down.'

Sara did so, tucking her legs neatly under the chair. She looked around. 'Your office looks very professional and productive. I hope I'm not disturbing you too much. What do you do, exactly? Emma told me this is an engineering firm, but there are all kinds of engineering.'

Alex sat down on the corner of his desk, one leg resting on the floor. He seemed uncannily close to her, and Sara was hopeful that he didn't notice he was disturbing her composure. She'd never experienced anything similar before. She didn't know him, and had no reason to think he was the least interested in her beyond casual friendship. His whole personal situation was too complicated for someone like herself, who was just getting over a failed relationship. She explained it away by thinking that she was probably just very susceptible to any kind of emotional attraction at present. She concentrated on his voice.

'You're right there. Engineering covers a wide range of things. Construction, electrical, mechanical, mining, sound, aeronautical — the list goes on and on. At some stage in their training most engineers specialize in one particular area. My company still takes on individual jobs, but over the last couple of years I've started to build up a team of young engineers. I now tender for nearly everything that needs to be done under the same roof. We're capable of creating the working systems of new offices, blocks of flats, hospitals, schools, or shopping centres. We don't build them or have much say in the architectural side of things, but we'll take on the rest. We're still a relatively small firm and I want to keep it that way. I don't want to become a mega-concern where I don't know the people who work for me. I want good engineers who cooperate among themselves to produce the best and quickest financial results. We have to be a team of people who get on well with each other, and don't have delusions of individual grandeur. Generally we do things like the electrics, air conditioning, heating, ventilation, water system, lifts or even simple problems like figuring out the right position for emergency exits. Our all-round concept sometimes gives us an edge over individual companies who tender for just part of the work.'

'It sounds interesting, but getting those kinds of commissions must be difficult.'

He nodded. 'John and I — that chap

over there in the corner — put our backs into it, and Pam handles the administrative side of things. She's a qualified engineer too, just like all the others.'

'Sounds simple, but I bet it isn't.' Sara felt slightly breathless as she looked at him.

He laughed softly. 'No, it isn't. You have to be clued in to get a steady stream of commissions. My engineers expect good pay, and a month soon whizzes around when you're paying them. It's a balancing act all the time, but it's interesting and stimulating.'

'What about advertising? Do you use some, or a lot, or is it all word of mouth?'

'Not completely word of mouth, but reputation does play an important role. I haven't bothered much with public relations or advertising yet. It all costs extra, and we're still establishing ourselves.'

'But it's an absolute necessity! Corporate identity, web design, and an easily identifiable logo can make all the difference these days. Do you have one? A logo?'

He scratched his head. 'Not really. I've used the same heading for our letters and offers ever since I started.'

'Well it's about time you got yourself a new one. One that people will remember. A logo, a good informative website, and printed matter that hits you between the eyes. All modern companies need them these days.'

He laughed and gave her an irresistible grin that sent her pulse winging. She began to understand why his wife or any other woman before her had fallen for this man.

'I'll think about it.'

Pam interrupted them with the pile of pages. 'I've put a couple of empty pages back and front to keep them in good shape.'

Sara smiled at her. 'Many thanks. That was fast!'

'Laser printers *are* fast. Would you like a folder to put it in?' She looked at

Alex with a twinkle in her eye. 'I'm sure my boss will have no objection.'

Sara shook her head. 'That's kind of you, but if I put it carefully in the boot of the car, I'm sure it'll survive the journey back unscathed.'

Pam nodded and left them.

Sara stood up. 'That's it, then. Thanks again, Alex. I'm sure Veronica will be delighted with this. Are you sure you won't accept a donation towards printing costs?'

'No.' He reached for his soft jacket and a scarf from a neighbouring chair. 'But I hope you'll join me for a cup of coffee and a Danish pastry. There's a tea shop not far from here.'

A little flummoxed, Sara was wordless for a second. Alex rolled his sleeves down and slipped into his jacket. An unexpected warm emotion surged through her. If he wanted to voluntarily spend time with her, she had no intention of refusing his offer. He interested her too much. 'That sounds tempting,' she said.

He gestured towards the open doorway. 'Then lead the way. You can dump that manuscript in your car, and we'll go in mine. I'll bring you back after.'

Sara nodded and wove her way between the desks in the outer office. She noticed that he paused by someone's desk on the way to tell him something, and that a couple of the men had grins on their faces as they passed. Sara had a moment to adjust, and was honest enough to admit her spirits soared at the prospect of spending a little time with Alex on her own.

* * *

They were in the small teashop in a matter of minutes. It was the sort of place that invited you to linger. A coffee machine made hissing and gurgling noises behind the counter. It was romantically shadowy, and warm and cosy; the owner was friendly; and there was a good choice of cakes and pastries in a glass display case. Though the shop was busy, they managed to grab a window table just as another customer and his companion were leaving.

Sara flung her bag over the back of her chair and took off her coat. Alex took it and deposited it with a multitude of others on some nearby wall-hooks. She sat down and looked around. Above them the ceiling was low-beamed, and the tables had bright checked tablecloths and festive floral centrepieces. She remarked, 'This is nice. Do you come here often? It's not far from your office, is it?'

'Closer than any other place. What would you like?'

'Coffee please, and the cheesecake looked tempting.'

He nodded and smiled. 'I'm a chocolate junkie myself, and they have a mouth-watering chocolate gateau.'

Sara laughed softly. The owner came to take their orders and then bustled off. Sara leaned back. 'Have you heard that someone stole some woodcarvings from the church? Emma told me this morning, and it sounds like the vicar's blaming himself because your local policeman's been trying to persuade him to lock the church at night for some time.'

Alex's dark eyebrows raised and he looked at her in surprise. 'No, it's news to me. I'm not completely surprised, though, because Paul only believes in the goodness of people. He finds it hard to accept the world is also full of cheats and criminals. I'm afraid I can't recall ever seeing any woodcarvings. I suppose a regular church-goer in the village knows what they look like, but I'm not one of them.'

'And yet you still got them the Christmas tree.'

'For Emma's sake.'

Their coffee and cake arrived, and they settled down in each other's company.

With a forkful of squashed chocolate cake on his fork, Alex asked, 'Have the police any idea who's responsible?'

'Not as far as I know. Emma was very put out. She's so involved in the village and church happenings, isn't she?'

'Emma and Paul get on like a house on fire. I'm surprised they don't realize it themselves and draw their own conclusions. It'd be good for them both if they tied the knot.'

Clearing her mouth, Sara sounded surprised. 'You mean get married?' She paused. 'I don't know either of them properly, but I know that they're both very friendly and helpful to each other and people in general. Emma does seem very involved in church happenings, so perhaps you're right. But there's more to marriage that just having similar aims and interests.'

'True, but I'm not the only one who thinks that way. Emma has a pronounced soft spot for Paul, and it's grown ever since his wife died. She manages to disguise it quite well most of the time, but she worries about him constantly. If you'd been here long, you'd notice how often she mentions

155

him. Anyway, I honestly think they do suit each other.'

'Do you realize you sound like an agony aunt? You told me the other day that you didn't appreciate nosey villagers, and now you're being one yourself.'

He laughed and flashed her a sudden smile that made him seem years younger. 'Am I? Perhaps it's because I like Emma and think she deserves some happiness.'

Sara nodded. 'I like her too. She's very sympathetic and always helpful.'

'Like you, then!'

She coloured. 'It only looks like that because I have time on my hands right now. When I'm working, I don't have much to spare. In town, most people don't know many other people.'

'That's a pity, isn't it? That's why I never wanted to live anywhere else but in the country.'

She tilted her head. 'But what about the nosey parkers? You said yourself not so long ago that it gets on your nerves.' She glanced out of the adjacent window. There were wisps of snowflakes dancing in the air. 'Oh, look, it's snowing. That's perfect.'

He followed her glance. 'Don't get too excited. It won't stick. They mentioned snow flurries on the radio this morning, but said the temperatures will rise again this afternoon. They haven't made a definite prognosis for Christmas Day yet.'

'A white Christmas would be perfect. I wonder what my parents are thinking as they sail through the Caribbean under lots of sunshine. I think it's the first time they've been out of the country at Christmas. They've been abroad for summer holidays, but never in winter.'

'They're either loving it or hating it, I expect. It's a new experience and that's important, no matter how old you are. You need to try something new all the time, otherwise there's no point in it all.' He hooked his cup and took a sip. 'What about you? Are you infatuated and in love with someone? I presume you're not, because you're spending Christmas here on your own, but there could be a perfectly logical explanation for that.'

Sara brushed the hair off her face and said matter-of-factly, 'I got my fingers burned quite recently, and I'm now glad I found out in time. He was having an affair with someone else right under my nose.' She shrugged. 'On the other hand, it was all for the best, because I now realize I didn't love him after all. Not in the way you should love someone if you want to stay together.'

He studied her thoughtfully for a moment. 'He must've been a very stupid man.'

Her breath quickened and a blush covered her cheek. Disconcerted, she looked out of the window for a moment while experiencing some perplexing emotions. 'It's all water under the bridge now, and I put it down to experience. It's made me think about looking for a new job. We worked in the same company so I'm bound to bump into him all the time. I'm not worried because I might still like him, I'm sure about that; it's just that I think it will be uncomfortable for other people who know us.'

'As long as you're not just running away from him because you can't live with the idea of losing him, that's okay. But if you have the slightest doubt and still like him, it might be worth another heart-to-heart talk about everything. You're right, a new start would be good for you.'

She shook her head determinedly. 'No, I'm sure I don't want him in my life anymore. If you can't trust some-one, there's no basis for a relationship, is there? Even if you stick a cracked plate back together, the crack is always there. That's how I feel about him.' She gave him a generous smile. 'You really are an agony aunt, aren't you?'

He laughed. 'Sometimes, perhaps. It's always easier to give other people tips and suggestions, isn't it? It's often more difficult to keep your own life on an even keel.' He glanced at his watch. 'I don't want to rush you, but I have a meeting this afternoon, so I must be getting back soon.' He added, 'I'd much rather prolong our chat, but that's how things go sometimes.'

She gestured to their empty plates. 'It's no problem, is it? We're both finished. I've solved Veronica's printing dilemma, and I've had a delicious break and some good conversation into the bargain. Let's go.' As their eyes met, Sara was caught off guard by a feeling that Alex was a man you could always trust. He was a man you could like. He was different.

He got up and helped her into her coat. Fumbling with his own coat, he went to the till and she followed. She offered to pay, but he brushed her words aside and ordered some cakes to take with him. As the owner was packing them, he explained, 'My sweetener for the others in the office, otherwise they'll start to complain about me dodging responsibilities and all the rest.'

Her eyes sparkled. 'It's your firm, isn't it? You can do what you like.'

He laughed. 'That's what everyone thinks, but you don't know my lot. They'd mow me down without a second thought.' He tucked his free hand under her elbow and she opened the door. The wind met them full force and they hurried back to his car. The snow flurries had stopped.

A few minutes later they were standing next to Sara's car again. 'Thanks, Alex, for the printed book and the delicious tea break,' she said.

'You're welcome. See you soon, I expect.'

She got into her Mini, and he went towards the building. He turned and lifted his hand before he disappeared inside. Sara started the engine and checked the mirror before she set off. Thinking about their talk, she realized they hadn't once mentioned Katie or his wife. She couldn't make up her mind if that was a good sign or a bad one.

9

Back at Emma's, Sara ran upstairs and left the manuscript in front of the Calderwood-Morrises' bedroom door on the way. Unzipping her boots, she spread-eagled herself on her bed and stared up at the ceiling. She wondered what Alex thought about her — not that it mattered, of course, but it intrigued and occupied her more than she wanted to admit. He was friendly and relaxed in her company, and sometimes she felt there was something unspoken in his dark eyes.

She was jogged out of her musings when her mobile rang. It took her a minute to find it in the muddle of her bag. 'Hello.'

'Sara? Rod here!' Sara took a deep breath, and it must have been audible. He hurried to continue. 'Look, don't hang up. Give me a chance to explain.

You rushed off without hearing what I needed to tell you.'

She felt her temper rising and snapped, 'There's nothing you can tell me that I don't already know.'

'Oh, bloody hell! I didn't want to hurt you, Sara. Somehow it got out of control.'

'If by 'it' you mean the affair you were having behind my back, yes I can imagine it was quite a juggling act. It wasn't even a one-off get-together, was it, Rod? It had been been going on for months, even long before we got together. Gilda put me in the picture, and I wish she'd done so a long time ago. The most difficult part for me to accept was that the affair was going on before we started going out together and you swindled me from day one until I finally found out.'

'You have to believe me. You meant too much to me, Sara. You still do. Francis was a slip-up. I tried ending it, but she kept clinging every time I tried, and I just gave in to her tantrums and weeping instead of finishing it like I should have.'

'Then I can only pity Francis and be glad I found out in time. There's a saying about papering the world with good intentions, isn't there? I'm just not interested anymore, Rod. I could never trust you again. What we had was never meaningful. We were always looking for different things, weren't we? I wanted stability, and you wanted excitement and something new all the time.'

'Aw, come on Sara. I made a mistake. It'll never happen again. Promise!'

'Sorry, but I just don't believe you. I'm just not interested anymore. I hope one day you'll meet someone you like so much that you'll never think about cheating on her. I'll never be able to think of you now without remembering how you two-timed me.'

'Where are you? I'll join you. We can spend Christmas together. I'm sure we can sort it out if you give me a chance. I miss you, Sara.'

'No way! I don't miss you, Rod, so there's nothing to sort out. Please don't phone me again. There's no point in trying. Bye!' She cut the connection.

She left the phone where it was, pulled on her boots, and went downstairs again. Grabbing her coat and scarf from the hallstand, she went out for a brisk walk. Thinking about Rod made her all the more certain she needed to move on, and to find herself a new job.

The sun was trying to break through some grey clouds edged with silver. The sprinkling of snow had completely disappeared, and there wasn't even any frost on the ground at the moment. The skeleton branches of the trees and the bare-twigged hedging along the way suited her mood perfectly. After a couple of minutes she noticed Peter was coming towards her, returning from one of his excursions. It must have been a short one today, because it was still early afternoon.

When they drew closer, she asked,

'Going back? I needed some fresh air, but I've gone far enough. I'll turn and come back with you.'

He nodded. 'I took a short route this morning.' He adjusted his backpack and they set off again.

Sara looked at him and wondered why he was so quiet. Usually he was quite talkative whenever they met. 'Anything wrong?'

'No, not really. I've been thinking about my former girlfriend. How I believed we were suited, and how she dumped me for someone who had more money and social standing.'

Sara dug her hands into her pockets and buried her chin from the oncoming wind in her collar. 'Isn't it better to find out than to make a big mistake? There's no point in telling yourself that things are all right when they're falling apart, is there? I found out in time and I'm glad that I did.'

'But if I had more money, a bigger house, a holiday home — all the things this other chap has — she might come back. We got on like a house on fire and liked the same things until she met him. I don't understand it.'

'But there must've been something amiss in your relationship, otherwise it wouldn't have gone wrong. It sounds like the financial side of things was more important to her than you thought. Excuse me for saying so, but you don't seem to be hard up. If the attraction of still more money with someone else was the main reason she left you, she must be very materialistic. She was bound to meet other men with more money or more possessions in the course of time. Even if you managed to talk her round again now, you can never be sure that the same thing wouldn't happen again one day in the future.'

Sounding gritty, he muttered, 'I was prepared to do anything to get her back, and I thought if I had more money it would solve everything. I know you're right, though, and I have to accept the fact she's gone — but it's not easy. My gran used to say there's no point in whipping a dead horse. You're saying that too, in another way, and I know you're right.'

Sara smiled. 'That's the spirit. When you've had more time to look at it objectively, you'll find it easier to accept. Who knows, perhaps there's someone much nicer for you just around the corner. That's what your gran would tell you too, I bet.'

Peter pushed his glasses back into place and nodded. 'Yes. The trouble is, you do the wrong things for what you believe to be the right reasons and find out you can't turn the clock back to put them right afterwards.'

Sara didn't quite follow what he was talking about, but thought it was important not to meddle in his personal business too much. He was intelligent enough to add up the pros and cons on his own. She nodded silently and they went on.

He began to talk about some birds of prey he'd watched out on the moor. By the time they reached Emma's he seemed more relaxed, and she'd also shoved the memory of Rod's telephone call out of her thoughts completely.

Emma was back and looking flustered.

'Hi, Emma. What's wrong? Have the police found any clues?' Sara turned to Peter and explained about the stolen carvings.

His eyebrows drew into a straight line and he looked down for a moment. 'Really? That's shocking, especially when it happens in a small place like this. Something you'd never expect. Nothing is safe these days, is it?' He looked at his watch. 'If you'll excuse me, I promised to phone someone. I must dash.' He turned away, shoved his walking shoes under the hallstand, and then took the stairs two at a time.

Sara was surprised. Generally he was too polite and interested in goings-on to rush off. She watched him disappear and decided that their conversation about his ex-girlfriend hadn't cleared the air. He was taking her rejection hard. Sara was glad that she didn't have that kind of problem, and it also emphasised how little she'd really cared about Rod.

Emma said, 'The police are doubtful we'll ever see them again. No one even knows exactly how old they are. We all took them for granted. Paul said the police told him that once they land on the black market, they'll end up in someone's private collection.'

'It's awful, but you can't do anything except hope the police will find them.'

Emma looked troubled. 'The detectives tramped around in the church this morning, looking for clues. It doesn't seem right, policemen in our church. I've just come from there. They pulled things about and I had to rearrange some of the decorations.' She looked at her watch. 'Well, I'm going to prepare something for this evening's meal now. I've promised to take the chair in the Christmas meeting of the Women's Institute this afternoon and read Paul's speech to them. He has to report to his bishop to talk about the theft. I think he's nervous, in case the bishop reproaches him about being too easy-going with church security.'

Sara nodded understandingly. Emma's forehead creased as her thoughts ran on. 'I've got to fit fetching Katie from school into my schedule too. I can always slip out from the meeting and take her back with me for a while. The other women won't mind. I suppose I could phone one of the other mothers and ask her to take care of her until it ends.' She looked speculatively at Sara, and her eyes twinkled as she thought about an alternative solution. 'Or, if you're not doing anything special this afternoon, will you do me a great favour and fetch her? Katie knows you and likes you. If you bring her home, it'd mean she's where Alex expects to find her. I don't like bothering you, Sara, but it'd be one less worry off my mind.'

Sara smiled at her. 'I'll fetch her, it's no problem. But please phone Alex and tell him.'

'Yes, I'll do that,' Emma said, returning the smile. 'I promised Katie I'd take her on the bus to buy a Christmas present for her dad, but I'll do that with her sometime tomorrow.'

'I'll take her if you like. If Katie expects to buy something for Alex this afternoon, she'll be terribly disappointed if she doesn't.'

Emma looked startled. 'Oh! I couldn't expect you to do that too.'

'I'd like to, honestly. I wouldn't offer otherwise.'

Emma gave her a quick hug. 'You're a good girl.'

'Get on with you! I'm enjoying myself.'

'That's a load off my mind. We're going to put the tree up in the living room tonight. When that's in place, I always have the feeling Christmas is almost here at last. I asked Ken to get me one and he brought it last night. I need something to cheer me up. Ken thinks he won't be here on Christmas day because of those rich friends of his.'

She looked away. 'He still doesn't know if he'll be going to the south of France. He said he wanted to get away from all the fuss here and spend the day basking in the sun.'

'He'll need to be very lucky to do that. It's not always as warm as you might think there, at this time of year. One day he'll find out that Christmas at home is something special. Perhaps he'll settle down with a nice partner somewhere locally and surprise you with how his priorities have changed.'

'He'll need to change a lot to catch a local woman. For a start, he needs to stop spending so much money. I don't know where it all comes from.' Sara was thinking the same, but didn't say so. 'I love him, but I'm not blind to his faults. I just hope he'll wake up to reality one day.'

Sara threw her arm around Emma's shoulders and propelled her in the direction of the kitchen. 'Make whatever you intended to and get that out of the way. Why not do something like spaghetti bolognese? That's filling, and you'll only need to cook the spaghetti later on.'

'A good idea, but I don't have any fresh minced beef.'

'Where's the nearest butcher's? You can start chopping the onions and tomatoes and so on, and I'll get the meat. How much do you need?'

Emma smiled. 'They have it pre-packed in the village shop. I've bought it there before and it's quite good.'

Sara grabbed her coat and called back over her shoulders, 'Don't forget to phone Alex and get his permission.'

'I won't. I'll put the kettle on, and we can have a quick mince pie and some coffee when you come back.'

Ten minutes later, Sara was back, and they chatted while Emma did her preparations for the evening meal.

Sara heard the Calderwood-Morrises returning and went to tell Veronica about the manuscript in front of their bedroom door. She beamed her thanks, and even Roland looked happy. He was clearly very supportive of Veronica's efforts, and Sara was pleased.

In fact, helping and being part of other people's lives gave her a very satisfying feeling. She'd never had much of a chance to help anyone in her own neighbourhood the last couple of years, apart from Mimi. She'd done Mimi's shopping and taxied her around a couple of times after her hip operation. She didn't know the names of most of the others living nearby, or what they did. But here in the village it was a functioning community, and it was quite normal to help other people if needed. She was able to help because she was on holiday, and people were always grateful. Belonging and helping were firmly rooted in local custom.

Emma hurried off after preparing the evening meal, stating she'd be back in plenty of time to serve it up. She'd checked with Alex and he had no objections to Katie being with Sara.

Sara read a couple of chapters of a novel before it was time to go the school. At the appointed time, she stood outside with a group of other mothers waiting to collect the first-year pupils. Some of them greeted her with a friendly smile, or said hello, and others huddled together in their chosen cluster and ignored everyone else. The bell rang on time, and minutes later the children began to pour out of the main door. Sara wasn't practised in picking out one little girl in amongst the whirling mass, so she didn't spot her straight away. Katie spotted her, though, and came across smiling.

Sara explained about Emma, that her dad had agreed she could pick her up, and that Emma approved of them shopping for Alex's present. Katie whooped. Sara noticed Megan Butler standing in the doorway watching, and when she noticed Sara, she looked mystified. Sara took Katie's hand and thought an explanation should be on the board. Megan was responsible for the children and Sara was a new face to the village.

After she'd explained about Emma,

Megan responded with a strained expression. 'It wasn't necessary to get you involved. Alex knows my number and he knows I'm willing to take care of Katie any time, any place.'

'I expect Emma and Alex thought you've looked after all the children long enough for one day,' Sara said. 'I don't mind. I'm looking forward to our shopping excursion.'

Megan's eyes were cool. 'I still think Alex could've asked. We're friends — good friends. He knows it's no trouble.'

Sara smiled and tried to soothe ruffled feathers. 'Oh, you know what men are like. I'm sure there was no offence intended.'

From her expression, Megan still wasn't mollified. 'I don't want to be rude, but someone who's a visitor to the village doesn't know Katie and Alex as well as I do. I would've enjoyed going shopping with Katie.'

Sara didn't intend to bicker with Megan about something so insignificant. She was clearly resentful, and Sara wondered why. Was she was jealous? There didn't seem any other explanation for her reaction. Well if that was the reason, it was silly. Sara had only arrived a couple of days ago and she'd be gone in another week. Alex certainly didn't think of her in any kind of romantic way.

She shrugged and decided not to prolong the conversation. 'Come on, Katie. Let's go. We'll go to that café in the market square, and you can have some hot chocolate and tell me what you'd like to buy for your dad. Do you have an idea yet?'

Katie shook her head.

'We'll find something, I'm sure.'

In town, they sat at a table that someone had just vacated overlooking the street. While they waited for their order, they watched the people in the square and looked at the sparkle and arches of lights everywhere. Katie chatted about her day at school and what they'd done. They both had hot chocolate and muffins and then set out on their search.

10

They had a good time together. Katie chatted nonstop. Sara had to keep hold of her hand among the crowds. The little girl was clearly anxious to find the perfect Christmas present for her dad. She handed Sara a small purse with what she had to spend, and Sara grinned when she saw the pile of coins. They sat discussing what they could buy. Sara knew it wouldn't please Alex if she financed an expensive gift out of her own pocket, so she tried to think of something that wasn't too dear.

'What about a nice photo frame? I'm sure Emma has a picture of you to put in it, and I'm sure your dad would love it for his desk in the office. Or a tool, perhaps, like a screwdriver? Or does he like chocolate? You could buy him some of that with your money. A nice magazine about something he's interested in, perhaps? A pair of warm socks? Aftershave?'

Katie thought carefully for a moment. 'A photo frame — that'd be nice. He could choose which photo to put in it himself, couldn't he?'

'Jolly good idea.' Sara smiled. 'What about your other friends? Or your grans and granddads?'

'I'm going to draw them pictures.'

Sara nodded. 'And Emma? Does she get something too?'

Katie looked more apprehensive. 'I could give her a picture, but I'd like to buy something. Will I have enough money?'

'It depends. I think you might manage a pair of woollen gloves or a box of chocolates, something like that.'

Katie beamed. 'Gloves! Red ones. She has a nice red scarf, and she said a little while ago that she'd like a pair of gloves to go with it.'

'Then that's what we'll get her.' Sara reached out for her hand, and they fought their way between the other

Christmas shoppers.

Sara found that, unnoticed by Katie, the little girl was reproducing the magic of Christmas again for herself. Katie's innocent excitement, her pleasure in buying something for people she loved, the hustle and bustle — it all reawakened memories of her own childhood.

Katie chatted and Sara listened as they went from shop to shop looking for the perfect gifts. On impulse she bought Emma a cookbook because she knew how much Emma loved cooking, a bottle of good wine for the Calderwood-Morrises, and a small book about local history for Peter. If they were getting a Christmas tree, they needed a few parcels underneath to make it look genuine.

By the time they were finished, the daylight had faded and they were glad to get back to Sara's car for the homeward journey. She presumed that Alex would come to pick Katie up from Emma's as usual, so she drove there.

During the journey, Katie related how Father Christmas was coming to the school tomorrow, and that they would break up for the holidays afterward.

'That sounds exciting. I'm surprised that Father Christmas has time to come. He must be very, very busy at the moment sorting out everyone's Christmas presents and packing his sleigh. It's only a couple of days till Christmas.'

From the back seat, Katie explained, 'Dad said he probably had business to clear up near here before Christmas, so maybe he had time fit it in. Perhaps he's picking up toys from a nearby factory?'

Looking at her eager face in the rear-view mirror, Sara hoped the illusion of Father Christmas wouldn't be shattered too soon. 'Perhaps. Is he bringing any presents tomorrow?'

'Miss Butler says she doesn't know, but we shouldn't expect anything too big if he does. He's not coming with his reindeers and sleigh. I wonder if he's coming by taxi?'

Smiling, Sara said, 'Perhaps one of the farmers will give him a lift in a horse and cart. I can imagine he's never used a taxi. He's just not used to them.'

'I'm not scared of taxis. Me and Dad went in one to the airport last year.'

'Did you? Where did you go?'

'We went to Spain. We had a bungalow right next to the beach. It was super!'

'Wow! I bet it was.'

The lights were burning everywhere when they reached home. Katie dashed inside, wanting to tell Emma about their outing. They found everyone in the living room with Emma, busy decorating the big lush tree standing next to the fireplace. There were cardboard boxes all around full of shiny red balls, sparkling silver chains, small colourful figures and lot of other bits and pieces.

Roland was kneeling, trying to straighten the tree. With his head covered by some of the lower branches, he uttered to no one in particular, 'If it's not straight, there's no point in decorating, is there? It'll fall over.' Satisfied, he got up. 'That's better.' Rubbing his hands together, he added, 'Covered in resin now, but nothing a bit of scouring power won't remove.' He saw Sara and Katie and said, 'Hello, you two. Come to help?'

Veronica stood nearby, watching. Her face was animated and her eyes lively. She looked like a different person to when she arrived.

Sara asked, 'Have you sent it off?'

She nodded. 'It won't get there until after Christmas, and might go straight into the slush pile; but even if they don't like it, someone might be kind enough to take a look and give me a few tips about how and where to improve.'

'That's the spirit.' Sara took her coat off and helped Katie out of hers. 'Your son chose a lovely tree, Emma. It's quiet majestic.' There was a strong smell of fir in the room.

'Yes, I think so too. We haven't had

one as big as this for a couple of years. It must've been expensive. Ken bought a new car a few weeks ago, and now he's off to the south of France. I don't know where he gets all the money from.' Her brow furrowed as her brain wandered through the possibilities.

Katie eyed the tall tree and her squeaky voice asked, 'Can I help to decorate it, Emma?'

'Of course, love. Here — you can hang these balls and some of the figures on the bottom branches. Sara, Veronica and I will do the middle — and perhaps you'll get the household steps from the pantry, Roland, and hang things at the top?'

Everyone was in agreement, and a few minutes later, when Peter joined them with a book in his hand, there was an untidy scene of unpacked decorations and all of them thronging around the tree, thoroughly enjoying the task in hand. Peter looked on and had to grin. There was no room for him to join in even if he'd wanted to, so Emma suggested he fetch the bottle of sherry, some orange juice, and a plate of mince pies she'd put ready on the dresser in the kitchen.

When Alex arrived, they'd finished decorating and were standing around admiring their finished handiwork. His eyes twinkled when he viewed the crowd of people who were complete strangers a couple of days ago. How did Emma manage it? She had a knack for bringing people together. As his glance skimmed them all, he paused when he looked at Sara. And there was something extra-special about her too.

Katie spotted him and flew to his arms. 'Look, daddy, isn't it beautiful? The most beautiful tree in the whole world.'

He kissed her forehead. 'I agree. It's sensational.' He met Sara's eyes and winked.

'Why haven't we got a tree like this?' Katie asked.

'Because we won't be home much. We're going to spend Christmas Day with both grans and granddads, and we're coming to Emma's on Boxing Day.'

Sara's heartbeat accelerated at the news. Katie was a little appeased and nodded. Sara thought it was a shame Katie and Alex only had a small artificial tree at home, but she could understand why. She handed him a glass of sherry and a mince pie on a paper serviette. 'Here, join us. We're celebrating already.'

'As I'm almost home, I will.' He took a generous bite of the mince pie and it almost disappeared. 'Um! Nothing can beat Emma's. The best! All we need now is some snow, some Christmas music, and someone to fetch Scrooge to celebrate with us, and then it'd be almost perfect.'

'Who's Scrooge, Daddy?'

Alex looked over her head at Sara and answered, 'I'll explain later. He's a character in a Christmas story. I'll tell it to you before you go to bed. Okay? I'll finish work early tomorrow and come to pick you up from school.'

'Father Christmas is coming to school tomorrow.'

'I know — you're already told me about a hundred times. Some people get all the luck!'

Sara viewed his tall figure and lean face and thought how quickly she'd grown to like him. He'd seemed so reserved and solemn at first, but she knew now that it was just a protective mask in front of strangers. He wasn't easily steamrolled by anyone. That was why she had a warm feeling when she thought how he'd now accepted her into his world.

He let Katie slide to the floor and looked at his watch. 'Time for us to go, young lady. We have to prepare a meal and you have to go to bed. If Father Christmas is coming to school tomorrow, you need to be on your toes and on your best behaviour, or he might change his mind about bringing something for you on Christmas Day. Put your coat on and thank Sara for taking care of you. I hear you wanted to do your Christmas shopping?'

Katie grabbed the plastic bag and hid it behind her back. 'Don't look. It's secret!'

He laughed softly. 'I won't.' He glanced around. 'I must tell Emma that I'll pick you up from school tomorrow. Where is she?'

Sara said, 'I think she's gone to the kitchen to start the evening meal.'

Alex went searching for her, and Sara helped Katie with her coat and bobble hat. She heard Emma and Alex talking in the hallway, and the dialogue increased in volume and sounded very animated. She wondered if something was wrong. Alex and Emma were usually the best of friends. She slipped out and closed the door behind her.

Emma was gesturing and trying to persuade him. 'The police are insisting that Paul take a look at a catalogue of carvings they're borrowing from some ecclesiastical museum tomorrow, so that they have an idea of exactly what they should look for. He doesn't know how long it'll take, and he's worried he'll let the children down. You have the afternoon off anyway.'

The look on his face was one of horror. 'But not to dress up as Santa Claus for Katie's school class! I haven't a clue what to do! I can only remember seeing Father Christmas once — that was last year when I took Katie to that department store. I was too busy taking a photo to notice what he said, or anything else. I think he was an old man — I'm thirty-two!'

'You're good with children, and they sense that. You only have to ask them some questions about whether they've been good, what they want for Christmas, and pretend to check things or write in your book. You say a few words now and then, and then give them their present. That's what Paul does and the kids love it.'

Alex ran a hand through his thick hair. 'Emma, you know I always try to help you if I can, but this is going a bit too far. I am *not* Father Christmas.'

Sara had to stop herself from laughing. He looked so overwhelmed and confounded.

Emma adjusted her tone to sound repentant. 'I know I'm asking a lot of you, but I wouldn't do it if I could think of someone else who was suitable and available. Harry used to do it, but his rheumatics have got so bad he can't cope with standing for so long. Janet's husband is the right size, but he's on duty. We need someone who's tall and available. We don't have time to alter the costume; we'd have to take the whole hem off and re-sew it. Normally I'd do it if I had enough time, but I'll be so grateful if I don't have to start sewing again tonight. The costume will fit you; Paul is roughly the same size. Please, Alex! I'll never ask you to do it again, I promise.'

'Have you considered that Katie will recognize me — that's if I consent to do it?'

'If you keep your head down and you

muffle into your beard when you talk to her, she won't. Don't look directly at her. Try to disguise your voice, and wear gloves.'

He at Sara with a very worried expression.

Emma didn't stop. '*Please*, Alex! Paul is terribly worried that he'll let the children down. He's upset enough already because of the robbery.'

After a moment he said, 'Oh, all right. I'll do it for Paul. But never, never ask me to do anything like this again! I swear I'll refuse outright. There's a limit to what I'm prepared to do. I don't like making a fool of myself.'

Emma gave him a friendly clap on his arm. 'You won't. Who's going to recognize you? Thanks, lad. The presents are all packed and waiting in the school. They're just trifles like pencils, notebooks and the like. I'll fetch the costume from Paul tonight and you can pick it up anytime tomorrow. Be at the school by four at the latest, and go in by the back door so no one sees you. I'll phone Megan and tell her about the change of plans, and I'll remind her to leave the door unlocked.'

'What about Katie? She's expecting me to be in the audience, and once the antics are all over she'll be expecting to find me waiting for her outside afterwards.'

'She'll be too engrossed with what's going on when she's inside. The kids have to sit together at the front of the room. Get out of your costume sharpish when it finishes; they usually sing a carol when Father Christmas leaves. Get changed and then tear around to the front to meet her as fast as you can.' She looked across at Sara. 'Perhaps Sara will go along to divert Katie when she comes out. She can distract her till you turn up.'

Muttering to himself as he realized what he'd got into, Alex nodded; and with a more worried expression on his face than when he arrived, he went into the living room to collect Katie.

Sara looked at Emma and burst out

laughing. 'Emma! You are the absolute limit.'

Emma nodded and joined in. 'I know, but I wouldn't put him in a spot like this unless I could find someone else at short notice. I'll never ask him to do it again. We'll have to organize an official stand-in for future emergencies, just in case. There are a couple of pensioners who might do it, if I give them time to get used to the idea.'

Emma's eyes were twinkling, and their combined laughter echoed through the hallway. Sara hoped Alex couldn't hear them. That would put the cat among the pigeons. She couldn't wait to see the outcome of it all tomorrow.

11

Sara went for a walk the next morning. She went part of the way with Peter. There was a flurry of snowflakes, and she tipped her face to enjoy the feeling as they melted on her face. The snow silenced any other sounds.

There was a little boy ahead of her, pulling a sledge along the pavement. It grated as he dragged it along. The layer of snow wasn't thick enough by far, but he was determined. He disappeared down a lane, and she heard the sound of other children playing somewhere nearby.

The sky was a lead-grey colour and the clouds were busily charging across the heavens. Generally Sara only noticed such things on her way to work or going home, and even then the sky was always hedged in above all the buildings. But here the fields stretched to the horizon and there was space all around. She was more aware of nature now than she had been for ages.

Peter was starting out on one of his longer treks, and when he turned off before the start of the village, she went to buy a newspaper and then returned to Emma's. For the rest of the morning she had a relaxing time reading. Emma was out somewhere, presumably with Paul or doing something to help him in the community. Sara looked out of the window and wondered if the older woman realized how involved she was with Paul's work, and he with her. There was truth in what Alex had said about the two of them.

Daylight had almost disappeared by the time she put on her duffle coat and thick winter boots. Her parents had always taught her to be punctual, and it was now an ingrained habit. She decided to set off in plenty of time. She was surprised when she opened the door and found Alex.

He eyed her with approval. 'Would

you like a lift to the school? Emma said you'd agreed to come.'

'That'd be lovely. Are you nervous?'

'Don't ask! I still don't know why I let myself agree to this. There must be someone else around who's better suited.'

'You're doing it to help Emma, and I'm sure you'll manage it with aplomb. You're already used to small children. There may be some cheeky, loud or shy ones among them, but you'll cope.'

'I'm glad you think so. I'm not so sure.' With a sweeping gesture, he motioned her to his car, and they drove the short distance to the school.

There weren't as many cars around this afternoon because the older children had already gone home. The teachers probably didn't want them around to spoil the fun of the little ones, who still believed in Father Christmas and the magic of the festivities.

'I'll just show myself and talk to Katie, then I'll do a disappearing act and go around the back. I've been told to appear when I hear them singing 'Rudolph the Red-Nosed Reindeer'. Heaven help me — I can't remember when I last felt so nervous.'

'You'll be fine.'

They went inside and Sara hesitated at the back of the room, watching as various parents or grandparents went to exchange a few words with the children. The kids were all excited, and there was a buzz of conversation. They were all looking around in the hope of seeing Father Christmas somewhere. Alex bent to say something to Katie, and she nodded animatedly. She was soon busy talking to her fellow pupils, and Alex faded towards the back of the room again. He hurried to his car for the costume and came back.

Sara decided to give him some moral support. She waited for him outside and nodded at him, asking quietly, 'Manage the costume on your own?'

He shrugged. 'I hope so.'

'I'll come with you. Perhaps two of us

can manage things better than one.'

He didn't protest. He nodded and they slipped around to the back of the school. The door was slightly open and they went inside. He unpacked the bulky red-and-white coat with its attached hood and thick leather belt from the bag onto a nearby table. He was wearing a thick navy pullover and dark trousers underneath his own outdoor coat. He shrugged his way into the outfit and found it fit well lengthwise. After tightening the leather belt, his day shoes were barely visible. He pulled out the white curly wig with its attached white beard from the bag.

Sara wanted to giggle, but she knew that would be counterproductive, so she managed to contain her amusement and look attentive.

Tugging the beard into place, the result was very effective. Alex looked around quickly. 'If there was a mirror in this place, I could check myself. Is it okay? Somehow I don't believe that Father Christmas has white hair, a white beard, and black eyebrows.'

'You look very impressive. I don't suppose they'll notice such a small detail.'

With dry amusement in his voice, he said, 'Clearly you underestimate some kids!'

Sara saw there was a small tin still in the bag. She rattled it. There were some pins and hair clips inside. 'Look — if you put up your hood, I'll fix it more securely so that it won't fall off. That would be a catastrophe.'

Alex smiled. 'Okay.' He pulled the bright red hood with its white border into position, and Sara started to pin it on strategic points.

She'd never been so close to Alex before, and his nearness was suddenly overwhelming. She cleared her throat, concentrated on what she was doing, and pretended not to be affected. She felt the heat from his body, and her pulse leapt with excitement. Her communication skills suddenly plummeted to zero, and his steady gaze bored into her. He watched her intently as she worked. There was a lump at the back of her throat, and when his gaze met hers, her breath was uneven and her limbs felt unsteady. She fumbled as she fixed the last pin and stepped back, lurching to the side as she did so.

His hand shot out to prevent her stumbling, and there was a moment of silence that seemed like an eternity as they stared at each other. Finally, he pulled her closer, wrenched the beard under his chin out of the way and kissed her. She felt the heady sensation of his lips, and his kiss was more persuasive than she cared to admit. It sent a shockwave through her body. Her emotions whirled and skidded. She could see, and hear by the intake of his breath, that he was also bowled over.

Coming back to earth with a bang, they both realized someone was knocking at the connecting door to the classroom. Sara stared at Alex, tongue-tied, and he kissed her again quickly. This time it was surprisingly gentle and she found herself kissing him back, savouring every moment.

With one last look at her, he pulled his beard into place and said, 'That wasn't planned, but I'm not sorry.' He grabbed a bulging jute sack standing next to the door, and they heard the children beginning to sing 'Rudolph the Red-Nosed Reindeer'.

Still confused by what had just happened, Sara noted in a haze how he hoisted the sack onto his shoulders. She managed to move out of sight behind the door so no one could see her. A wave of excited singing and voices enfolded Alex as he entered the classroom.

The door closed behind him, and she was left to run her fingers over her lips and come to terms with the knowledge that Alex had kissed her and said he wasn't sorry he'd done it. It was completely unexpected, and she exhaled a sigh of contentment. She wanted to be with him; a hidden magnetism drew her to him no matter how hard she tried to ignore it. He was someone special, and the attraction grew stronger every time they met. It should be a fairly straightforward situation, but it wasn't. It would be if it were just the two of them, but there was also the memory of his wife, and the way he adored his daughter. Katie wasn't really a problem; it would be easy to love her. But if the little girl realized she might have to share her daddy with someone else, would she rebel — and could Sara cope with that? She reminded herself that she'd be leaving the village after New Year's. Perhaps what had just happened was only Alex out looking for an adventure, with no strings attached? He was young, attractive, and had his desires.

She pulled herself together and stepped outside into the cold winter air, then thrust her hands into her pockets and made her way around the building and in through the main door again. She stood at the back in the shadows.

Her thoughts were still in turmoil. She was only partly aware of what happened up front. Concentrating, she watched Alex talking to one of the little boys, and decided he was coping well. The children were nearly all impressed by his presence and sat quietly. Some were waiting expectantly for their turn; others looked like they hoped it would be over soon.

Sara still managed to take some photos. Alex stood each child on a chair so that they could look at his face. He managed to deepen his voice whenever he spoke. When it was Katie's turn to face him, she didn't seem bothered that Father Christmas mumbled and kept his face towards the floor the whole time. She accepted her gift in its bright paper wrappings, said thank you, and hurried back to her seat to unpack the coloured pencils.

The time passed in a bit of a haze for Sara. She found it hard to concentrate on the present happenings. By the time the children began clapping and singing

'Jingle Bells', she still hadn't decided what her next move should be.

The children and their various carers at the back of the class began to get ready for leaving, and there was a general sound of children wishing each other and Megan Butler a merry Christmas. Sara made her way to the front, near to where Katie was saying goodbye to one of her friends, and watched them indulgently. There was a lull in the activity, and Sara found Megan Butler was standing next to her. Feeling obliged to comment, she remarked, 'It went off well. I think the children were all happy with Father Christmas, don't you?'

Megan viewed her with a cool expression. 'I didn't realize you were here again, Miss Holden.'

Noticing the formality of 'Miss Holden', and checking that none of the children were close enough to hear, she answered, 'Emma and Alex asked me to come, to keep an eye on Katie until he's changed and can join us.'

With single-minded intent and a determined voice, Megan responded, 'What a waste of your time. I'm here and I could've kept Katie occupied until he was ready. He only had to ask. Emma told me last night that Alex was coming, and I presumed he'd get in touch, but he didn't.'

Beginning to feel a little riled by the other woman's attitude, Sara said, 'I don't know why he didn't, or why he asked me to come instead. I was just doing him a favour.'

'You seem to be doing him a lot of favours recently, don't you?'

'Perhaps. Does that matter?'

'When I think about Alex's problems over the last three years, and how he doggedly remained independent and refused help all the time, it makes me wonder if you've given him the wrong idea, or a misleading impression. You're a visitor. Why should he involve you in his life when there are enough other people, like myself, who are too willing to help?'

'Ask him, not me. I haven't given him any kind of wrong impression. Why should I?' With heightened colour, she continued, 'Are you insinuating that I'm trying to attract Alex? I can assure you I'm not. I like him and we get on well, but I have no romantic aspirations. As you so rightly remarked, I'm just a visitor.' She couldn't help adding, 'If the way he acts bothers you so much, perhaps you have ambitions of your own? If so, take my advice and don't pressure him into anything. It'll only have the opposite effect.'

Megan's eyes sparkled angrily. 'If I want your advice, I'll ask for it.'

Sara didn't answer. She looked around for Katie and caught her eye. Calling her, she said, 'Come on, Katie. Your dad's gone outside to look for you. We didn't notice you were saying goodbye to your friends after Father Christmas left, and he thought you might've slipped outside.'

Katie skipped across and shoved her hand into Sara's. 'Did you see him? Did you see Father Christmas? Wasn't he super?'

Sara banished Megan Butler from her thoughts. 'Yes, great. Let's go and find your dad now. He'll be worried if he still can't find you.'

Katie grabbed her coat from the back of a nearby chair and, with her newly acquired pencils in the other, they made their way into the playground in front of the main doorway. Sara knew she should have encouraged Katie to wish Megan Butler a merry Christmas, but she didn't. Either Katie wanted to do it of her own free will, or not. Sara had no intention of meeting Megan Butler again this afternoon. The teacher was clearly jealous of any other woman who was a hair's breadth from Alex.

With Katie at her side, they wound their way through the throng of people who were saying goodbye before finally leaving for home. Sara noticed Alex coming towards them. He'd spotted them, and it was easy to spot him because he was tall enough to stand out in a crowd. She began to feel slightly embarrassed and her cheeks burned. She was angry with herself for feeling confused and having dangerous thoughts just from looking at him. They stood waiting, and he made his way through the crowd, exchanging a word with someone here and there. When he reached them, they stared at each other across a sudden silence, and his dark eyes held Sara's mixed-up expression.

Katie prattled on about her chat to Father Christmas. She drew their attention away from each other and towards her eager face. Alex lifted her up and held her tight. Her eyes were level with his and she continued to describe the afternoon's excitement. He nodded and smiled. The white of his teeth flashed in the fading daylight. When Katie finally paused for a moment, he took the opportunity to say, 'That was enough excitement for one day. Let's go home. I'm on holiday now, you're on holiday, and Christmas is just two days away.'

'Hurrah! Now that I've told Father Christmas what I want for Christmas, I'm sure he'll bring it for me.'

Sara managed to clear her throat long enough to ask, 'What did you tell him you want?'

'A doll's house. One like I saw in a big shop when me and Daddy were together in Bristol one day.'

Sara nodded, conscious of Alex's every glance in her direction. 'I'll keep my fingers crossed. But don't be too disappointed if you don't get exactly that one. Remember that he has to give presents to hundreds and thousands of boys and girls, and sometimes there just isn't enough time for everyone to get exactly what they wished for. Sometimes things get mixed up.'

Alex added, 'Come on, let's go. The car's just down the road. I was getting worried because I couldn't find you.'

Katie giggled. 'Sara told me that. You know I wouldn't go anywhere unless I was with someone I knew. You keep telling me not to do anything silly.'

They set off side by side. Sara found that despite everything, there was nothing she could do to fight the overwhelming feeling of happiness to be here with Alex and his daughter. Her heart jolted and her pulse pounded away as she thought about how his kiss had removed any doubts about how she felt. It was easy to pretend to Megan Butler that he meant nothing to her, but in fact she couldn't stop dreaming about being crushed in his arms and feeling his kisses again. She tried to forget the kind of uncontrolled emotions that made her senses spin. She had never experienced something so powerful and all-consuming before, and they had only met a couple of days ago. The feelings she'd had for Rod faded to nonexistence in comparison.

She tried to be sensible and remind herself that it was a stupid, slippery path she was on, and it would lead nowhere. Alex liked her, but that meant next to nothing, and there was certainly no reason to think something worthwhile and stable would develop between them apart from a short friendship and some fleeting kisses. Love, the kind Sara hoped to find, didn't happen that fast, and certainly not when various obstacles and hurdles lay ahead. With her heart pounding as she secretly peeked at Alex's profile in the semi-darkness of the car, she told herself to be sensible.

Katie chattered happily about Christmas and was looking forward to telling Emma what had happened. Sara and Alex were unusually quiet, but Katie didn't notice. When they drew up in front of Emma's house, Alex began to help Katie out of the back seat. She then ran up the path and through the door to look for Emma.

Sara tried to calm her emotions and looked at Alex's unreadable features. The wind played with his hair as he stood with his hands in his pockets. With a playful expression, he said, 'We need to talk about what happened earlier.'

Sara felt like a breathless girl of eighteen. Just the sound of his voice affected her in a way she'd never experienced before. She managed to swallow a lump in her throat and meet his gaze. It wasn't easy to hide her feelings, but she tried. 'Don't worry, Alex. I didn't pick up the wrong signals. I understand. These things happen.' She felt increasingly uneasy under his scrutiny.

His expression steadied and he looked puzzled. 'That's all it meant to you?'

Sara opened her mouth. She was at a loss to know what to say, but just then Emma came out, motioned them in, and made her answer superfluous. 'Come on, you two. Katie's already started to tell me all about this afternoon.' Her eyes twinkled when she said, 'It seems that Father Christmas was a huge success.'

Alex turned away abruptly and strode determinedly up the path. Sara followed in his footsteps. Once she was inside, she took off her coat; and while Alex and Katie went off down the corridor after Emma, she took flight and ran up the stairs, two at a time.

In the haven of her room, she threw herself onto the bed, trying to calm her thoughts and think things through while holding back some silly threatening tears.

12

What did Alex think about her? Perhaps she was making too much of it. It was just a kiss. Perhaps it was only a sign of his friendship, for helping Katie with various things during the last couple of days.

Her thoughts circled endlessly. This afternoon had just complicated the situation. She'd try to remain uninvolved so that when she left here she could pick up the threads of her previous life again without a snag. She hadn't finished with Rod just to get involved with someone else on the rebound. She needed time to sort herself out and re-adjust. Alex was attractive and she liked him a lot. Perhaps if they'd met years ago, when he was free, she'd have liked him enough to admit openly that she wanted more.

When she checked the time, she was surprised how late it was, and hurried to freshen up for the evening meal. Downstairs the others were already in the dining room, and soon she joined them.

Emma bustled in with slices of fresh bread, butter and a selection of sausages and cheeses for starters. Arranging things on the table, she said, 'Italian food this evening. Baked chicken and pasta next, and tiramisu for dessert.' She looked at Sara. 'Alex and Katie wanted to say cheerio, but you disappeared.'

Sara felt some faint colour spread across her cheeks. 'Did they? Father Christmas was a great success, but I don't think you'll ever get him to do it again.'

'Father Christmas?' Veronica asked.

Emma left, and all of them helped themselves to the food. Between bites of crispy buttered bread covered in slices of fragrant salami, Sara explained that Alex had stepped into the breach to help Paul, who was busy with the police investigation.

Roland nodded. 'Jolly decent of him. Emma told us about how someone stole some things from the church. What's the world coming to, I wonder. Who'd sink so low that they would steal from a church? What exactly did they steal? Candlesticks, that sort of thing?'

'No, some wooden carvings,' Sara answered. 'They were hanging on the wall near the altar and depicted the life of Jesus. No one even knows how old they were.'

Touching his moustache with the corner of his serviette, Roland said, 'Perhaps the vicar was asking for trouble when he didn't lock up, knowing how things are these days. A miracle that they haven't disappeared before now, if you ask me.'

Sara shrugged. 'I suppose so, but I expect everyone thought that sort of thing happens elsewhere, not here. Apparently the local policeman has been trying to persuade Paul to lock it overnight for ages.'

Roland nodded. 'If someone plans to steal something, they'll find a way. Day or night, it doesn't matter. The surrounding graveyard is big with lots of trees and bushes; they block the view from the road. Veronica and I wanted to look around the church but the police were busy inside, checking things. Have you been there, Peter?'

'Me? Er . . . no I haven't, actually. I've been meaning to, but I've always set out across the fields before you get to the village.' He reached for another slice of crusty bread and took time deliberating which cheese to take, then cut a piece of Camembert and asked, 'I presume these carvings are valuable? How valuable, I wonder?'

Roland reflected for a moment. 'Haven't heard, and I'm not into history. Any idea, Veronica?'

She was getting used to being included in the conversation. 'I haven't seen them, so it's hard to guess. They must be ancient, and that alone makes them priceless. Centuries ago most people couldn't read, so coloured windows, altar carvings and the like made the Bible more tangible for them. This is a small place, and wasn't rich enough to have elaborate church possessions, but someone like the lord of the manor must've donated the carvings. They're items that are easy to transport. On the black market they'll fetch a decent price because of their age. If they're by a well-known carver, they'll fetch a lot.'

'But someone, somewhere might recognize them, won't they?' Sara shifted in her seat.

'Once someone buys them via the black market, they'll often end up hidden away in a private collection. Some people build special rooms so that they can gloat in solitary enjoyment.'

'It's dreadful,' Sara said. 'Stealing something that has hung peacefully, probably for centuries, on the walls of a village church.'

Emma came in with the pasta and the conversation rambled on. Sara looked forward to a few hours in the sitting room with the others. The Christmas tree and the other decorations heightened the seasonal atmosphere, and everyone was growing more attuned to each other with every passing day. Just two days to go. Sara had never been a regular churchgoer, but this year she thought seriously about attending the midnight service.

She needed to go to town again tomorrow, even though she had hoped to avoid any last-minute shopping. Now she knew that Katie would be coming to Emma's on Boxing Day, she wanted a suitable present. She intended to give her own gifts to the others on Boxing Day too, to make it more enjoyable on the whole for Katie.

Later, when she mentioned her plans for Katie to the others, she discovered that that they had also bought her small presents. Even Peter. She noted they'd become a kind of small community, even though they'd drift part forever again in a few days' time. They all agreed to postpone the present-giving until Boxing Day when Katie was there.

★ ★ ★

The next morning, Sara hurried through breakfast. She didn't want to admit she wanted to avoid Alex, if he happened to call. She pretended she wanted to avoid the last-minute shopping in town.

Once she was on the way, she relaxed. The sky was a dull lead colour, there was no wind, and it had rained during the night. It was also cold — cold enough to accentuate the delights of Christmas articles in the shop windows. She'd already decided to get some doll's furniture for Katie. Even if Katie didn't get the much-longed-for doll's house, she had enough imagination to use them for other games.

It was still early when she arrived, and the streets were eerily quiet. Last night's showers still mirrored the surface of the pavements. Sara wondered if they would be icy, but apparently it wasn't cold enough for that. Nearly all the shops weren't open yet, and there was a definite atmosphere of a 'calm before the storm'. She noticed there seemed to be an unusual number of men around. Most of them had puzzled and worried faces.

She headed for the town's only department store. Because she'd visited the town a couple of times already, she now had a rough idea of where to find it. She walked down narrow alleyways towards the main square, past half-timbered buildings with undersized windows and off-line profiles, and resisted the temptation to look for a café — she'd think about that once she'd achieved her goal. Killing time by looking in the window displays on the way, Sara soon noticed the number of shoppers was increasing. By the time she reached the department store, it was just due to open. There was a small crowd waiting patiently in front of the entrance. She joined them.

She found several boxed sets of plastic furniture. Sara thought about her own doll's house and looked in vain for nicer furniture made of wood. She remembered seeing a small old-fashioned toyshop down a side street and decided to check there first, before she bought something she didn't really like. No doubt most little girls wouldn't mind if the furniture was pink and white plastic, but she did.

To her delight, in the other shop she found pieces that were more expensive than their plastic counterparts, but in her eyes far more attractive. She calculated quickly and bought a couple of items that could be used in any room. Satisfied, and clutching her packed parcel, she dodged other shoppers and set out for a nearby café.

Almost there, Sara looked up and saw Peter coming towards her. This must be one of his short-hike days. She smiled at him but noticed his expression was decidedly downcast. His face lightened a tad when he saw her, but he still looked depressed. Sara wondered what was wrong.

When they drew level, she asked, 'What are you doing here? Last-minute shopping, like me?'

He shook his head. 'Just drifting.' Absent-mindedly, he considered her and then said, 'I'm glad I've met you like this. Have you a moment to spare?'

'I was just about to go for coffee. Come with me. There's a nice little place just round the corner.'

He nodded and walked alongside her. The café was comparatively quiet, although some tables were already occupied. They went to a vacant one in a corner niche. Sara hung her coat on a convenient hook in the wall and tugged off her scarf. Peter unzipped his anorak and sat down opposite.

'They have some super pastries,' she said. 'Want to indulge yourself?'

He shook his head. A waitress appeared and they both ordered coffee.

'Well? What's bothering you? I can tell something's wrong. Has Roland dropped more negative remarks about guys who work in the city?' She smiled and hoped it would help.

He shook his head. 'No, in fact I think he's improved a lot. He's okay when you get to know him better.'

'If it isn't that, what's the problem?'

'The carvings from the church.'

She was puzzled. 'The carvings? What do you mean?'

'Can I trust you?'

'I hope so.' Jokingly she continued, 'If you've pinched them, I'll have to think again.'

He ran his hand over his face and said quietly, 'That's just what I've done.'

Shock and amazement were written on Sara's face. She had a moment to recover when their tired-looking waitress arrived with their steaming coffee cups. After she left, Sara lowered her voice and felt sensible enough to say, 'You mean you stole them?'

He nodded.

'But why?'

He shook his head in despair. 'Remember that day I told you about how I thought my girlfriend might come back if I had more money? That was just after I did it. After I'd taken them, I realized straight away that it was one of the stupidest things I've ever done in my life. I wanted to replace them on the double straight after I'd taken them from the wall, but at that moment I heard someone in the vestry. I panicked and left the church as fast as I could. I hoped I'd be able to put them back later that night, but I didn't reckon that someone would notice the loss so fast. When the vicar discovered they were missing, everything went ballistic. I don't know what to do now, apart from giving myself up to the police.'

Sara bit her lip, not knowing what to say.

'That day I met you, I managed to tell you I thought I would've kept my girlfriend if I'd had more money — because I already wanted you to understand why I did it; but I didn't have enough nerve to tell you I'd already stolen them. I just want to put things right. But how? If I give them back to the vicar, he might be compassionate, but he might be forced to hand me over to the police. He'd need to explain where they came from. The church is locked at night, and there are always people around there during the daytime. There's no chance of putting them back unnoticed anymore.'

'Where are they? In your room?'

He shook his head. 'In the boot of my car. I feel like I'm transporting a dead body around with me all the time.'

'I bet. I don't condone what you've done, but I'm trying hard to under-stand why you did it. You have to find a way to put them back without anyone knowing.' Sara stirred her cup listlessly and tried to think of an easy solution.

'It's no good me trying to slip them back, as I'm a stranger too. Any visitor stands out like a sore thumb in the village, especially anywhere near the church. You can't involve Emma; she's too close to Paul. It's better she doesn't know, because she'd be pulled in two directions. Knowing her, she'd want to help you put things right, but she'd have to lie to Paul and I don't think she'd do that.'

'No, I don't want to involve her either. Emma is a super person. That's one of the reasons I came back here this Christmas. Roland would expect me to go to the police straight away. He's definitely on the side of law and order.' He paused for a moment. 'Not that he isn't right, of course. I was so stupid. You were the only person I could think of who might be able to suggest something. I'm sorry to burden you with it all, but if you can't help me to think of a way out, then I have no alternative than to admit it to the police. I acted like a fool; I know that now. If I hadn't heard the noise in the vestry, I would've put them back on the wall and they'd still be there now.'

Out of curiosity, Sara had to ask, 'Do you actually know people who sell stolen goods?'

He ran his hand down his face. 'Of course not. I didn't think that far, about the technicalities of what I'd do when I had them. I just thought about a chance to get some extra money.'

She met his worried expression. 'How big are they?'

He showed the width and the length with his hands. 'They're not very big. They fit in my backpack easily.'

Sara shoved her hair off her face and took a deep breath. 'Gosh! This is such a surprise. I need time to think about it. I'm making myself just as accountable, aren't I.'

'I don't want to put you at risk. I only hoped you could think of a way to put things right.'

She shook her head. 'Not off the cuff. I'd like to help, Peter, because I honestly believe that you panicked. Give me some time, okay?'

He nodded and reached across the table to cover her hand with his. 'You don't know how much of a relief it is to talk to someone about it. Thanks for that, no matter what happens.'

'Don't despair yet. Perhaps there's a way out. Give me a little time to mull things over before you do anything else. I suppose you could pack them up and send them by post, but there's always a danger of the police tracing where they came from and finding out who posted the parcel. There are so many cameras around everywhere these days.'

'I hadn't even thought of that! If I can't think of a better way, at least that's a possibility.'

Sara got up. 'We'll talk again later.'

*   ★   ★

On her way back to Emma's, Sara glanced out of the window at the flat spreading fields separated from the road by straggling hedges. There were grey and purple shadows in the folds and hollows everywhere. But the pleasant scenery didn't divert her thoughts from Peter and the carvings. She wanted to help because she honestly believed he wasn't a bad character. He'd done wrong because he'd trusted and believed a woman who didn't deserve his loyalty.

The car radio continued to play Christmas jingles nonstop this morning, but she sought a solution that would work. It took no time at all until her thoughts focused on Alex. He was the only person she trusted enough to ask for advice. She didn't know anyone else in the village, apart from Emma and Janet; but even if she'd known them all, she would have still turned to Alex with her problems. The more she thought about the situation, the more convinced she was that he was the only person she could confide in, and who might be prepared to help. He'd mentioned yesterday that he wouldn't be working this morning. If she were lucky, he'd be home now.

She drove past Emma's house and turned into Alex's driveway. She was relieved to find that his car was in front of the garage and that he didn't seem to have any other visitors.

13

With her heart in her mouth, Sara rang the doorbell and waited. This was the last place she expected to be today, especially after she'd more or less resolved to avoid Alex as much as she could for the rest of her stay.

She heard his heavy footsteps, and then when he opened the door he couldn't have looked more surprised. He had a tea towel flung over one shoulder, and as soon as he saw her his expression settled to one of cool detachment. Sara found she didn't like the idea that flitted across her brain that he wasn't happy to see her. She pushed it aside and concentrated on her aim.

'Sara? What can I do for you?' With a slight edge of sarcasm to his voice, he continued, 'As you made every effort to avoid me last night, I wasn't expecting to see much of you again, certainly not this morning.'

Her voice sounded as nervous as she felt. 'I wasn't deliberately avoiding you.' She crossed her fingers behind her back and hoped some higher deity wouldn't punish her for lying. 'I went upstairs to change, and it was so warm and comfortable I just fell asleep on the bed.'

She knew from his expression and the tone of his voice that he didn't believe her. 'Very convenient, I'm sure. In the car it wasn't possible to talk because of Katie and her elephant ears. Afterwards, you chose to disappear. I'm not stupid, and as you plainly have no interest in me and mine, I can only apologize if I made you feel uncomfortable.'

She felt flustered, but not about the previous day. She didn't like the way he was turning her into the villain of the plot. 'Don't be so pompous, Alex.' He stiffened slightly and his eyes sparked dangerously. Colour flooded her cheeks. 'Granted, I was surprised when we ended up kissing each other, but it wasn't entirely your fault. I'm a big girl now and I'm old enough to resist when someone gets close and I don't like it. I didn't do that, did I?'

As their eyes met, she felt a shock run through her. She wondered why that happened all the time now, but was relieved that he sounded more appeased when he said, 'I gather you have a problem with the fact that I'm a widower with a daughter, but I thought you could cope with that and we could move on from there.'

She shoved her hair back off her face. 'Alex, I've just stumbled out of a failed relationship, and I'm not sure if I can trust my own judgement properly at the moment. Admittedly I was surprised when we kissed yesterday, because everyone suggested you're still grieving, and haven't had any interest in anyone else since your wife died.'

He studied her coolly with bland eyes. 'I hadn't, until yesterday.'

Sara swallowed hard, and there was a moment of stillness. She hesitated, torn by conflicting emotions, before she remembered why she was here and tried to order her thoughts. 'I'm sorry if I offended you; that wasn't my intention. I'm flattered, but I need to talk to you about something else. I didn't come to talk about us; that'll have to wait. Can I come in out of the cold for a couple of minutes?' She looked over his shoulder. 'Where's Katie? I hope she's not listening to this. She'll put two and two together and make five.'

Alex smiled. 'She counts very well.' His expression steadied and he gestured vaguely. 'She's upstairs somewhere, listening to stories on her player.'

'And — can we talk? Indoors if possible?' Sara fidgeted with the strap of her bag and waited.

He was suddenly aware she was still standing outside. 'I'm sorry. Of course, come in!'

She did, and cautioned herself that

this wasn't the moment to sort out what he thought about her. She was here on a mission — to help Peter, if she could. She wondered why every time she was near this man, the sensible side of her character flew out the window.

Alex slapped the tea towel on his hip. 'Go through to the sitting room; you know where it is. Give me your coat.'

She did so and went ahead of him. Winter sunshine flooded the room, and she liked the brightness and clear lines. It needed some soft touches here and there, but the basic impression was elegant. Most of the furniture was modern, but a touch of timelessness was achieved by the inclusion of a beautiful old writing desk.

Alex gestured to one of the chairs, and she sat down. 'So if you didn't come to talk about us, what else?'

She took a deep breath and looked up at how he stood tall in front of her with his long-fingered hands in his pockets. His jeans skimmed his lean hips, and a faded blue work shirt turned him into the embodiment of the kind of modern-day romantic hero she read about in books sometimes. She shook herself and forced her thoughts onto the task in hand.

'I'm hoping I can trust you not to repeat what I'm going to tell you, even if you decide not to help.'

Puzzled, he waited.

'It's about the carvings from the church.'

He nodded. 'What about them?'

Sara told him. When she finished, he whistled. Intense astonishment settled on his face. 'Peter? The chap I met the other day? Whatever made him do a stupid thing like that?'

'From what I gather, his ex-girlfriend rejected him a little while ago, and he thought that if he had more money he'd be able to entice her back. It was a spontaneous act, so he says, and I believe him. He's not the type to steal something from a village church. He's a banker in the city.'

Alex lifted his dark eyebrows. 'Bankers are like any other people. There are probably just as many criminals among them as in other levels of society.'

'I know, but I don't think Peter is one of them. He's too ordinary. Someone whose main love is daylong hiking isn't the kind of person who'd steal things from a quiet country church. I think he just acted crazily because he was desperate to get his girlfriend back. He hadn't even thought about what to do with the carvings once they were in his possession. He said he immediately realized it was a stupid move. He was about to put them back when he panicked after he heard noises in the vestry. If he'd only then taken them back out of his rucksack and just left them on the floor, or told whoever it was that he'd only taken them off the wall for a closer examination, they would have probably given him a telling-off, but at least he wouldn't have got himself into this pickle.'

Alex stared at her, baffled, and then

239

ran his hand over his chin. 'And how am I supposed to help? You realize I don't approve of your attempts to help, or excuse, him. Not for a second. He's not an immature juvenile with whacky ideas. He was stealing.'

'He knows he's done wrong and he just wants to put things right. He swears he's never been in any trouble before, and I believe him. He'll never forget it. I don't mean just about stealing the carvings. I mean he realizes that trying to hang on to his misplaced trust in someone who didn't feel the same for him has just landed him a vat of boiling oil.'

'And? What's it got to do with me?'

Sara paused and smiled tentatively. 'I'm hoping you'll put them back in the church for him without anyone noticing.'

Staring blankly with his mouth open, Alex bit his lip to stifle a grin and then threw back his head, laughing loudly. 'You want to make me an accomplice?'

'If Peter or I tried to put them back,

someone in the village would notice us, especially after what's happened. He's already thought about doing it, but the church is locked at night now, and any strangers wandering around the church or the churchyard in daylight would be conspicuous. Someone local wouldn't get the same attention. It'd only take a couple of minutes. There's no need to hang them up. It'd be enough to put them by the altar and get out fast.'

His grin was irresistible, and Sara could tell the idea fascinated him. 'Do you realize what you're asking me to do?' he said. 'The police are looking for these carvings, Paul is frantic because he thinks it's all his fault, and Emma spends most of her time trying to pacify Paul and helping him keep up with his Christmas activities. This is one of his busiest times.'

'I know. That's why I don't want to involve Paul or Emma. I think they'd both be kind and compassionate, but it'd mean they'd have to lie to the police.'

241

'And you think it doesn't matter if you and I abet your Peter? It's criminal!'

'Please, Alex! He's not 'my' Peter. He's just someone who's done something he regrets. It's Christmas, and if we don't help him he's going to end up in jail. He says if I can't come up with a solution, he intends to go to the police and confess everything.'

'Humph! So he's passed the buck on to you and put you on the spot.'

'He's probably so desperate that he can't think straight about anything anymore. I know it's a dicey situation, but I couldn't think of anyone else I could turn to. The only other thing I can think of is parcelling up the carvings and sending them by post, but the police have methods of checking paper, writing, ink, fingerprints, traces of DNA on things like stamps, and they have cameras in all kinds of places these days.'

Alex turned to look out of the window. After a short pause he said, 'I'll have to think about it. As far as I remember Emma's description, they're not very big.' After a moment or two of further reflection, he added, 'I bought a pot of Christmas roses for Susan's grave this morning. I was going to take it there this afternoon, with Katie. The only idea I've got is to take her to my parents-in-law and pretend I've forgotten the flowers. Subsequently, I leave her with them, place the flowers on the grave, replace the carvings in the church, and then go back for Katie. The church is open all day, and if I met anyone I could make an excuse of checking that the tree was still safe. If I did, I won't be able to dump the carvings, and Peter will have to try your parcel idea or come out into the open and make a clean breast to the police. I can't think of any other way right now. I also promise you that I won't take the slightest risk. I wouldn't be able to talk my way out of it; my career would go straight down the drain, and I have to think of Katie.'

Sara's eyes shone. 'That sounds like a perfect solution.'

Alex forestalled any more of her words of relief. 'I haven't decided if I'll do it yet. I want to talk to your Peter first. I want to see what kind of character he is before I even consider helping him. You and I would be up to our necks in hot water if anyone found out we're involved.'

She tilted her head to the side and her eyes sparkled. 'But we know we're only being benevolent, sympathetic and kind.'

'And extremely stupid to even consider it.'

'Alex, it *is* Christmastime, and he's genuinely sorry. I don't want you to take a risk, of course not, but you can walk round the church and the churchyard without anyone taking much notice. I couldn't, and neither could Peter.'

He gave her a grudging nod. 'Okay, I'll talk to him.'

The door flew open and Katie rushed

in. 'Why didn't you tell me Sara was here, Daddy? Have you been out for a walk, Sara?' She came across and threw herself on Sara's lap. 'Want to see my bedroom?'

'Of course. Lead the way.'

While Katie showed her round her pink and white princess room, she mentioned she was going to the midnight service with Alex. 'Will you be there?'

Sara smiled. 'I'd like to. Isn't it very late for you to be up? If Father Christmas comes and you're not at home, what happens?'

'That's what's so exciting. I'm usually in bed by nine at the very latest. If Santa Claus comes, he'll find our stockings and everything ready. Daddy will only allow me to come if I promised to fall asleep straight after we get home, and not to get him up before my alarm rings.'

'Well, make sure you don't then.'

Silently Sara wondered if Katie would remember that. Pulling Alex out of bed at the crack of dawn was a picture that made her stomach tingle.

A few minutes later, Sara managed to escape with the promise of seeing Katie again soon. Helping her into her coat, Alex whispered in her ear, 'Send him round with the booty as soon as possible, so that I can decide one way or the other.'

Sara pulled her gloves on and said softly, 'I think he must be back at Emma's by now. He intended to wait and hope that I'd come up with another solution. I met him by chance this morning in town.'

Alex's smile was warm and genuine. 'Then put him out of his misery and send him round. And remember — if I do it I'm doing it for you, not for him.'

Unable to think of a suitable answer, Sara said, 'See you soon, Katie. And go to bed when you're told to, otherwise Father Christmas won't bring you anything.' She bent down to give Katie a hug, and kissed her forehead.

With Alex uttering softly, 'Some

people have all the luck,' Sara walked back to the car calmer than when she arrived.

How many men would have reacted to the situation like Alex had? He was considering the plan, despite his reservations about the rights and wrongs of doing so. It made Sara think it would be very easy to throw caution to the wind and think about a future with Alex Crossley.

When she returned to Emma's, she sent Peter around to see Alex. She quietened his fears about the fact that she'd been talking about what happened to someone else and explained that Alex would keep silent, even if he decided not to help. Peter's face was very tense when he set off down the road, a hunched figure. His backpack was clutched tightly in his hands, and his thin, solitary figure and bent head looked wretched.

Sara went to make herself tea to pass the time. Emma was out, and so were the Calderwood-Morrises. The tea grew cold and time dragged. When she heard the front door, Sara jumped up and met Peter in the hallway.

'And? What did he say?'

He looked slightly better. 'He's a brick! He's going to give it a try. I realize that if there's the slightest chance that someone else sees he's there, he'll break off and give me the carvings back again. But I'm so grateful to you both, no matter what happens. I don't deserve your help, although I'm praying that it'll work.'

Sara nodded. 'I'm sure that if anyone can do it, Alex can. But whether he succeeds or not, you must never tell anyone he and I were involved. That'd get us all into hot water.'

'I know. I'll never tell anyone, promise.'

'Good. Let's go into the living room and wait. I expect Alex will let us know one way or the other. There's a programme on about Lapland, and we have to fill in the time somehow. I made myself some tea, but it's cold now. I'll make us some fresh, and I'm sure Emma won't mind if I take a couple of mince pies to go with it.'

'I couldn't eat a thing, Sara. I'd be sick. I won't have a moment's peace until we hear from Alex.'

Sara stopped for a moment. 'I hope you haven't left any fingerprints on the carvings?'

'No; I rubbed them thoroughly, even the tiniest chink. Alex says he's going to give them another wipe-over to make sure.'

'Come on, then. We can't do anything more. We could go for a walk if you like?'

He shook his head. 'I want to be near the telephone.'

Sara patted his shoulder and thought about Alex. He was taking a chance for a complete stranger. He hadn't spoken to Peter, apart from just passing the time of day, until now. Sara sent up a silent prayer and hoped for the best.

Time dragged, and as the afternoon carried on, Sara could tell that Peter wasn't paying any attention to the TV. Daylight was beginning to fade when the sound of the telephone made them both jump. Sara looked at Peter and he nodded. 'You take it,' he said.

Sara lifted the receiver. 'Sara Holden at Emma Arber's house.'

'Sara? Alex. Tell him they're back where they belong.'

A hundredweight fell from her shoulders. 'Oh, that's just wonderful. I wish you were here. I'd kiss you.'

He laughed softly. 'Don't tempt me. Katie says you're coming to the midnight service. I'll see you then.' There was a chuckle. 'I'd like to be a fly on the wall when someone finds the carvings.' There was a click and the connection ended.

With almost a skip in her stride, she hurried back to tell Peter, who was waiting in the doorway. He'd gathered enough from the conversation to pick her up and swing her around before she could repeat anything. His face split into a wide smile. 'I can never thank you enough.'

'Don't thank me — Alex is the hero of the moment. Let's hope that when someone finds the carvings, the police won't make an effort to find out when they were replaced, or why.'

14

That evening, Peter kept exchanging pleased looks with Sara that showed her how relieved he was. He laughed at Roland's weak jokes and was visibly more relaxed with everyone as he joined in the table talk. Veronica and Roland had been into town and talked about the Christmas market. They were in good spirits too, so the meal passed very pleasantly.

Sara decided she would go to the Christmas service, and told herself it had nothing to do with the fact that Alex and Katie would be there. Before she went upstairs to change, she went to the kitchen to see if she could go with Emma.

When she opened the door, she found Emma with a shocked expression, sitting in one of the chairs. The kitchen smelt of cakes she'd been making for the days ahead. A tea cloth lay idle in her lap. It looked like she'd been in the process of clearing up when something had stunned her.

'Emma? Is something wrong? Has Ken had an accident?' It was the first thing that came to Sara's mind.

'No, no. Nothing like that, thank goodness. I'm just bowled over.'

'Why?'

'Paul just phoned a couple of minutes ago.'

'And?'

'He's just been to the church to put the lights on for the early arrivals, and to check that everything is in place for the service this evening. The missing carvings were lying in front of the altar!'

'The carvings?' Sara hoped she sounded suitably amazed. 'The stolen carvings?'

'Yes, isn't it wonderful? Almost like a Christmas miracle.'

'And where did they come from?'

Emma brightened noticeably. 'No one knows. Paul phoned around and asked people if they'd noticed anything unusual in the last twenty-four hours, but they hadn't. They weren't there when he locked up last night or this morning when he opened up again. Paul presumes some youngsters pinched them, had bad consciences, and finally decided to put them back where they belong.'

'If no one noticed anything, they must've been very cunning. Has he informed the police?'

'Yes, they sent some chap around to see if he could find any fingerprints. Poor man — on Christmas Eve too.'

Shifting on the spot, Sara asked, 'And did he find anything?'

'No. Clean as a whistle, so he said. We'll probably never know who was behind it. Paul is so relieved that they're back where they belong.'

Sara smiled. 'Yes. But I suppose it could always happen again. At least Paul's locking the church at night now, so that'll reduce the risk a little.'

Emma got up and began to bustle

around, clearing the remaining items from the table. 'Apparently they're very, very old. The police said that if they were similar to the ones Paul picked out from photos about church artefacts, they're quite unique. He'll have to do something about making them safer now.'

'How? If the church is open during the day, and I think Paul wants to keep it that way, anyone could walk in and do the same thing again.'

'The police suggested they should be wired to a burglar alarm that goes off as soon as someone tries to move them. It might put thieves off trying.' Emma sighed. 'That means we'll have to find the money somewhere. Church funds are always meagre and barely cover the upkeep now. Perhaps the local council will help, or a local business will donate towards it.'

'It sounds like that's the way to go. What about organizing jumble sales, that sort of thing? Churches often set up all sorts of auctions and sales when they need money to repair towers and so on.'

Emma's eyes sparkled. 'That's a good idea. I'll talk to Paul about it. I think he intends to keep the carvings in the vicarage until something's sorted out. There isn't a lot else of value in the church. Perhaps the candlesticks are an attraction, but he could always lock them away after the service so they're not on show to visitors.'

'Well it's good news, Emma. I'm sure the regular churchgoers will be pleased.'

'I'm sure they will, and Paul's absolutely delighted.'

Sara looked at her speculatively. 'You're very fond of him, aren't you?'

Emma busied herself with some baking trays and didn't look up. 'Yes, he's a good man. We're very, very lucky to have someone so dedicated to the village and to God.'

Sara didn't push her luck by asking too many questions. Emma was entitled to her privacy. 'I came to ask if I could come with you to the midnight service.'

Emma looked up. 'Yes, of course. We'll have to get there in plenty of time, otherwise we won't get a seat. The church is always packed at Christmas. It's a pity that people don't come on other days as well, but that's how it is these days. If we go from here just after eleven, we should be able to find a free corner somewhere. Do any of the others want to come?'

'I don't think so. No one said anything to me when I mentioned I was going.' Sara looked around. 'Can I help? Otherwise I'll go and read for a bit.'

Emma shook her head. 'Thanks, but everything's organized. We're having turkey tomorrow with all the trimmings, and on Boxing Day I've invited Paul as well as Alex and Katie. I'm not sure if Ken's left yet on holiday; he usually phones to say cheerio. If he's still at home, he might join us. I never know what he'll decide. He's inherited a lot from my husband; he's lovable but unpredictable.'

Sara smiled. 'We all have more of our ancestors in us than most of us imagine. My father often says I grow more like my mother the older I get!'

'Then I'm sure your mother is a very nice woman.'

Sara gave her a quick hug. 'I'm glad about the carvings.'

'Yes, so am I.'

★   ★   ★

The short walk to the church was invigorating in the cold air, and when they got there they found that the church was already packed.

The electric lights had been turned off and the church was wrapped in candlelight. There were a multitude of candles in the niches and along the altar steps, and very thick ones in several standing holders each side of the altar. There was a pungent smell of fir from the tree next to the door, and it mingled with the odour of the wax candles. Someone had added bowls of nutmeg and oranges pierced with cloves to the items already decorating the windowsills. The combined fragrances wafted around the building, and whenever traces of warmer air came within reach, it kissed the petals of a bank of red poinsettias in front of the crib. There was sparse heating in the old church, and Sara had her warmest boots on, but she could still feel them cooling rapidly as she squeezed in next to Emma in one of the ancient pews at the back of the chancel. Somehow Sara felt pleased that she'd been part of the preparations, and she thought back to the afternoon in the church when she'd helped Emma and Janet.

People kept arriving and the space in the small church filled fast. There was no more sitting room and the new arrivals had to be content with standing. Sara looked around for Alex and Katie and saw them among the crowd at the back. Organ music began to fill the church, and Sara met Alex's glance. She pointed at Katie and beckoned. He nodded and bent to whisper to Katie, who shoved her way determinedly through the throng and finally landed on Sara's lap.

Sara wasn't sure who was more entranced by the service. Katie looked enthralled and wound her hand around Sara's neck, snuggling up close. Sara noticed other children among the crowd, so Katie wasn't the only one who was up late tonight.

The service began, Paul's surplice startlingly white in the semi-darkness. He had a good voice that carried well, and didn't need a microphone. He told them the story of the birth of Jesus again and its meaning for people today. Carols that everyone knew and could sing broke up the various parts of the service, and when they did, the tune boomed back from the rafters and walls.

Towards the end, just before Paul gave his blessing and wished them all a merry Christmas, he mentioned that the stolen carvings had been returned to the church and how grateful he was. There was whispering and people clapped spontaneously.

The organ was still playing joyful music as everyone began to shuffle out. Lots of people waited outside to say goodbye to friends and acquaintances and wish them a happy Christmas. Paul hurried to the church doorway to add his personal farewells to his faithful and casual parishioners. Emma soon disappeared among the crowd, and Sara waited patiently with Katie. She nodded and smiled back at people who didn't know her, but who still greeted her and wished her well. Alex joined her, and Katie's eyes were bright and excited. Still holding Sara's hand, she took her daddy's hand too.

'Ready?' Alex nodded to some people passing who wished him a merry Christmas, saying, 'You too. Have a good one.' Turning his attention to Sara, and with Katie still jumping up and down and holding his hand tightly, he said, 'Merry Christmas, Sara.' He bent his head and kissed her on her cheek.

Sara felt confused for a moment before a faint blush spread across her cheeks. She was glad it was in the shadow where they stood and the people around them were busy. She hoped so, anyway. She wanted to reach up and touch the spot, and found that she longed for more than just a kiss on her cheek. Her heart jolted a little as she looked up into Alex's face, and there was a tingling in the pit of her stomach. She didn't understand why he of all men affected her like this. What she'd believed she'd felt for Rod was nothing in comparison to her feelings for this tall, ascetic man with his windswept hair and dark eyes — even though she'd only known him a few days, and they'd only kissed properly once. Had they been meant to meet, or was Christmas casting a spell that would go up in smoke when the decorations came down? She managed a 'Merry Christmas, Alex' before the momentary spell was broken by Katie's excited voice.

'It's snowing, it's snowing!' she exclaimed squeakily.

Alex and Sara smiled at each other and looked up. Katie was right. Thistledown flakes of snow were tumbling down at them. Light gusts of wind were hurling them around in an erratic dance, and when the wind died down they began to suddenly come down in a horizontal blur, looking for somewhere to land. The surroundings were quickly snow-streaked. It snowed faster and thicker by the minute, and if it continued at its present rate, tomorrow the land would be covered in a thick blanket of white.

Sara could only say, 'Perfect! What could be nicer than snow on Christmas Eve?'

Alex appraised her lazily and smiled. 'I can think of other things that would make it perfect, but we'll talk about that another time.' He grinned. 'I think we both have already made someone's Christmas perfect, haven't we? He'll sleep easier tonight.'

Sara smiled and nodded. 'That's thanks to you; I didn't have much to do with it. You took the risk, not me.'

'We were partners in crime. Luckily there was no one around, and I whipped in and out. I didn't see a soul.'

Katie was curious about the conversation and Alex noticed her puzzled expression. He knew she was sure to ask too many questions if they went on, so he said, 'Come on, Katie! It's time you were in bed. Say goodnight and merry Christmas to Sara.'

Katie was mollified. She did so, and was ready to go. She even yawned once, and Sara decided Alex wouldn't have much trouble putting her to bed now. With a final nod to Sara, he set off with Katie's hand enclosed firmly in his. Sara heard him and Katie greeting others on the way.

There was something about Alex that fascinated her and perplexed her at the same time. Her interest and attraction had grown so fast, in a way she'd never felt before. When she was with him she also felt so comfortable and relaxed. She longed for his kiss, for his touch — but was that wise? She wasn't looking for any more disenchantment.

15

The walk back with Emma through the village was exhilarating. The initial sprinkling of snow was now a real layer, and Sara thought that if it continued, tomorrow everything would look like a Victorian Christmas card. Houses were already lit up with Christmas decorations, and lots of villagers were still awake and probably filling stockings, packing presents and generally making preparations for tomorrow.

Sara and Emma parted in the hallway, and Sara made her preparations for bed with her mind still on Alex. A quick look out of the window before she climbed into bed confirmed that the surrounding landscape was already white. Winter had turned the grasses, gardens, barns and stone walls into a unified white. She just hoped that the temperature didn't rise suddenly tomorrow, otherwise a lot of children would be very disappointed. She watched the flakes drifting for a while. They looked like bits of silver in the lamplight shining from the corner of Emma's outhouse. It was a fairy-tale scene, beautiful and exciting. Children would see gnomes or other enchanted beings in the snow-covered hillocks and mounds tomorrow when they went out.

When Sara put out her light, sleep escaped her for a while. She put her hands behind her head and stared up at the ceiling. Was she reading too much into Alex's reaction and hints?

★　★　★

The next morning, the room was bright from the blanket of snow outside. It took a moment to register that it was still there. Sara jumped up and drew back the curtains. As far as she could see, the landscape was covered in snow. It wasn't snowing now, but everything was covered. Boughs of nearby trees were adorned with thick white pillows; and to make everything absolutely perfect while she looked, the church bells began to peal. Smiling to herself, she skipped back into bed, grabbed her phone, and checked the time before she rang her sister's number.

A drowsy voice responded on the other end. Sara could imagine what her sister looked like. 'Morning, sleepy-head. Merry Christmas! This is your beloved sister greeting you on Christmas Day.'

'Sara! Are you mad? Do you know what time it is?'

'I just looked. It's time for you and me to get up. What about Bob's parents? Don't they deserve a cup of tea in bed for once?'

Yawning loudly, Liz replied, 'Now that you've woken me, I suppose I could make an effort.'

Sara heard Bob mumbling in the background. 'Bring Bob one too while you're at it, and wish him a merry Christmas from me when he emerges.

It's too early to phone Mum and Dad — I'll do that just before lunch, if they haven't rung before then. Don't forget to phone them!'

'When do you intend to stop playing your 'big sister' role?'

'Never! That's my privilege. I'll open your present after breakfast. The packaging looks very grand.'

'I spent ages choosing it, so I hope you like it. Yours is at the bottom of our bed. I'll open it when I give Bob his. I'm not sure if he's bought me anything. I've searched his things but haven't found anything.'

Sara laughed. 'You'll never change! You never could wait. I'm surprised you've resisted the temptation to open mine. That must be the first time ever! Remember how you combed the house every year to find where Mum had things hidden? I think she left them with Gran to make sure you never found them.' Liz giggled on the other end of the phone. Looking at the white fields behind the house, Sara added, 'It snowed here last night. Everything looks absolutely gorgeous.'

'It did here too. I do hope it doesn't turn into that slushy kind of snow that turns the car floor into a mushy mess, don't you?'

'At the moment it looks like mashed potatoes here, with lovely stiff peaks. It's probably the perfect consistency for making a snowman. It's a pity that we all aren't together, isn't it? Perhaps next Christmas, eh?'

'You can bet your bottom dollar that Mum will insist on it. I do hope they're enjoying this cruise. You okay, Sara?'

Sara decided it was time to tell her about her break-up with Rod, and explained briefly what had happened. 'I'm perfectly okay, and I now realize I should've spotted the signs much earlier. I'm also absolutely sure now that I didn't love him after all.'

Liz was silent for a moment or two, then she said, 'I'm sorry. I wish you'd told me earlier. We could've gone to Spain or somewhere else together. Bob would've tagged along. He likes you. It wouldn't have bothered us to be together.'

'And I'm not bothered that I came here. In fact, I think it was the best thing that could've happened. Don't worry! I guessed you might change your own plans if you knew I was solo. That's why I didn't tell you earlier. Mum and Dad don't know yet either.'

'And you're definitely not lonely?'

'No, swear it! There's a nice crowd of people staying here, the village is a lovely place to be at this time of the year, and there's a promise of a scrumptious lunch ahead of us. I miss you and Mum and Dad, of course, but I'm having a good time. Much better than I expected.'

Sounding a little reassured, Liz said, 'Good. Phone me tomorrow, or the day after, and we can exchange Christmas gossip. Perhaps we can arrange to get together for New Year's Eve?'

'I've booked until after New Year's Day, but I'll think about it, okay? Don't worry; I'm fine. Just enjoy yourself! Love to Bob, and we'll talk again soon, promise.'

Sara shoved her phone in her bag and snuggled down into the warm bed again. It was still quiet in the house, and although she guessed that Emma might be up and already busy in the kitchen, she decided to laze a bit longer before joining the others.

When she eventually entered the dining room, Roland and Veronica were already at the breakfast table. Emma came in with a pot of fragrant coffee. They all exchanged smiles and Christmas greetings, and Emma warned them to leave plenty of room for lunch. She was going to church as soon as the turkey was in the oven. All the other preparations were finished, and the vegetables were also ready and waiting to be cooked.

When Peter joined them, he winked at Sara with a special knowing smile. She could tell he was still feeling terrific. He knew there was little chance that the real truth would ever come out now, especially if the police didn't have any fingerprints or any other clues to follow up on.

They all settled down in the sitting room after breakfast to laze away the morning, reading or watching the television. When Emma came back from the early-morning service, the clatter of preparations in the kitchen drifted to their ears. While Roland proceeded to pour them all a pre-lunch drink, Sara and Veronica agreed to help Emma. Veronica had instructions to set the table, and Sara to arrange some smoked salmon, bits of ricotta and greenery, and a delicious dab of creamy sauce on some of Emma's best china plates for starters. Emma was organizing the main course with all the trimmings, and a fat Christmas pudding was boiling in its linen cloth in the saucepan next to another saucepan with the ingredients for brandy sauce.

Emma joined them for the meal. Roland protested when he had to wear the paper hat from his Christmas cracker, but ultimately he gave in. Candles burning, a comfortable fire in the grate, some good wine, delicious food, and a festively decked table made them all feel good. Sara could only thank her lucky stars that she had chosen to come to Emma's.

They all helped to clear the table between the various courses, and even though there were pauses, by the time the pudding came in, covered in brandy sauce, everyone was beginning to protest and wonder if they could manage it. They did, and wished they'd been strong-willed and refused afterwards. Everyone felt bloated and overfed.

By the time the kitchen was cleared — and the women insisted that the men help — it was almost time for the Queen's speech, which Roland said he'd never missed apart from a couple of years when they'd been posted in some outlandish place that had no proper communications.

Sara leaned back in her chair and closed her eyes. Roland commented, 'Emma's a wonderful woman. She's done a first-class job.' No one disagreed with him.

Once that was over, everybody decided to look for their own bolthole where they would have time to digest the feast. Peter set off for a crisp walk across the moor and promised to be back in time for tea. The Calderwood-Morrises went to have a lie-down, and for once Emma said she was going to have forty winks too.

Sara wasn't tired, but didn't want to join Peter on one of his excursions because she guessed that he'd want to go much further than she'd enjoy. She decided on a stroll to the village and back. Suitably dressed, she set out. The air was fresh and chilly, despite the time of day, and the snow underfoot looked like it was likely to be around for a while. When she opened the front door, it lay crisp underfoot, and the cold hit her face as she took a deep breath of winter air. She thrust her gloved hands into her pockets and buried her chin in her scarf, then set off and was soon round the bend and almost on the empty stretch of countryside leading to the village. She couldn't help glancing at Alex's house when she went past. He was standing at the window and saw her. He waved.

Before she had time to react, he disappeared and reappeared at his door a minute later, beckoning to her. 'Sara, come in for a minute. This is the perfect chance for us to have a talk.'

She couldn't think of a plausible excuse fast enough, so she trudged up to the path. Gesturing her inside, Alex held out his hand for her coat and, after he'd hung it up, led the way into the living room.

16

Feeling nervous, Sara looked around.
'Where's Katie?'

'She's still with the two sets of grandparents, at my parents' home. She's thrilled to bits with her doll's house.'

'Is that what she got? Then I bet she's over the moon. I think that was her dearest wish.'

He nodded. 'She'd mentioned it to my mother several times, and so she told me. We saw one in a shop in Bristol once, and I couldn't get Katie away from the window for ages. I made a special journey to get exactly the same one. I took it with us this morning. I don't think she would've left the house without it. My parents and Susan's have bought furniture and other things for it, and the grandparents seem to be enjoying themselves as much as Katie is. I left them to it for a while.'

Sara nodded. 'I know Katie was hoping for one. She chatted about dolls' houses the whole time we were out shopping together.'

'The look on her face was priceless this morning, even if she did get me up at the first crack of dawn. It was worth every mile of the journey.'

Sara laughed. 'I thought she'd get you up early. I can remember how I felt on Christmas Day — you too, I expect.' Knowing that Katie wasn't around to interrupt them made her wonder if it was a good idea to be here with Alex alone. She hadn't sorted out her confusion about their relationship yet. She needed time to figure out what came next. 'What did you want to talk about?' she asked him.

'You can guess, can't you? I want to talk about us.' He stuck his hands into his pockets, and although he hid it well, Sara could tell he was nervous. Somehow that was reassuring. He wasn't taking anything for granted.

'Don't pretend you don't feel the attraction that's growing between us. If you say you don't, I won't believe you. Something's clicked between us ever since we met.'

Sara was almost panicky when she replied, 'You know that I've just ended a relationship, and I definitely didn't come here with the intention of starting another one. You, and your life, have enough complications in it without me.'

'Normally I'd agree with that, but I don't anymore. I'm in too deep emotionally, and I can't shut you out and forget about you as if we'd never met. I hope you feel the same way about me.'

Her lips were dry. She tried to tiptoe around an answer. 'I think it'd be better if we left things as they are. Don't try to analyse, or pretend, or force something. Neither of us wants to get hurt.'

His gaze took in her face. 'I'm not going to pretend or ignore the signs, and neither are you. If we ran away from the truth, we'd be cowards, and we're not.'

Before Sara could think of a suitable response, he smiled at her, which temporarily blocked any sensible thoughts she was trying to formulate. She tried to pull herself together. 'I'm not a helpless female, Alex, desperate for a relationship. Just before I came here, I was already toying with the prospect of changing my workplace, even moving abroad perhaps, with all the consequences that might bring. I'm not looking for complications.'

'You can't always control everything that crops up in your life. Sometimes you have to bend and compromise.' He brushed his fingers over her cheeks.

She bit her lip and tried to control her breathing. 'I've never believed in casual involvement, and I think anything more serious takes time.'

'That's one of the things I like about you. You're an all-or-nothing person. So am I. I'm not worried about how we'll get there at the moment. I only know that I want you in my life; it's as simple as that. I didn't think I'd ever fall in love again, but I liked you from the moment we met, and that liking has turned into love at a pace I didn't think was possible.'

Sara's heart hammered fast, and the quiet seriousness of what Alex had said made her insides melt and her mouth dissolve into a smile.

He felt encouraged to continue. 'I've been waiting and hoping you'd give me the right signals, but I sensed you needed some reassurance before you'd at least give me a chance. I understand why we need to talk things through before you can begin to trust me completely. Our situation isn't exactly run of the mill, is it?'

'I do trust you; of course I trust you. But . . . '

He put a finger over her lips. 'It's that 'but' again. There's never a right time or a right place to lose your heart, and I don't think we have much control over choosing the right person either. Come here.' He sat down, reached out for her and pulled her onto his lap. His nearness, the feel and the heat of his body, took her breath away. 'Somehow I think I need to tell you about Susan first, before we settle anything else. Am I right? You can be absolutely honest with me, because I understand why.'

Reluctantly, Sara bit her lip and nodded.

He settled her more comfortably and linked his hands around the back of her shoulders, drawing her even closer and making eye contact unavoidable. 'Susan was my first real love, and I'll never forget her. You have to accept that, because she was simply part of my past life. I see her in Katie now and then. We grew up together. We went to the same schools, shared the same circle of friends, and came back to the village after we'd qualified. We more or less drifted into marriage, but I did love her. She was a gentle, kind person, and we had a good marriage. Knowing that, I promise you she has nothing to do with what I feel for you, here and now. Susan left my life three years ago, and to be honest I never thought I'd ever meet someone I could love enough to replace her. I wasn't looking, wasn't expecting to find someone, and then you came along.'

Swallowing hard, Sara said softly, 'That's probably at the core of my dilemma. I don't want to be a replacement. I want to be the one and only. I'm worried in case you may unconsciously be looking for a substitute. We don't have a solid, unblemished basis for a relationship, do we? No matter how attracted to each we are.' He nodded, and Sara wished she didn't have such a strong urge to kiss his chin and then the rest of his face.

'I understand how you feel, and why. I shouldn't have used the word 'replace'. What I really want to say is, I hope you'll be my new beginning. I promise you that I have no intention of dwelling on the past, or ever making comparisons. I do understand that it might worry you. I'm someone with a past history, Sara, but so are you. What matters is what we feel for each other now. I'm hoping we'll find something strong enough to bind us together, in good times and in bad. Nothing in your past or mine matters once we stand together as one.' He ran his hand through his hair and it sprang back into place. Enfolding her within his grasp again, he went on. 'I don't come alone, and that's something that must be difficult for any new partner to deal with. I hope you're generous enough to accept Katie as if she belonged to us both. If you can manage that for my sake, I don't see any other obstacles. I'll do my damndest to make you happy. I want *us* to be happy, because I've come to believe we belong together.'

'Alex! Katie's grandparents, your wife's parents and your parents — they live just a stone's throw away. People in the village all knew Susan, and they'd make comparisons. They could make my life hell and ruin any relationship. Gossips and troublemakers can be found anywhere.'

'I think Susan's parents already realize I'm attracted to you. They've never heard me, or Katie, talking about someone in the way we do about you, even though you've only been here a little while. They're nice people, and they want the best for Katie. I wouldn't ever cut my daughter off from them, they know that, and I think you also understand that completely. I'm sure that in her own way Katie loves you already, and although we do have a more complicated beginning than some other people, I'm sure we can cope with whatever comes. As for my parents, I'm positive they'll jump sky-high when they hear I'm seriously interested in another woman.'

'And the villagers? Megan Butler detests me already, although I haven't done a thing to upset her. Who knows what some of the others will think.'

Alex looked puzzled. 'Megan? Why?

What has she done?'

'She hasn't 'done' anything. She's just made it absolutely clear that she fancies you, and she doesn't like me coming between Katie and you. She's sending out clear smoke signals saying 'hands off Alex'.'

He threw back his head and laughed, then gave her a quick kiss. 'Megan's been throwing her cap at me since kindergarten. She just doesn't want to accept that I'm not interested in her, never have been, and never will be.'

'And the rest of the village?'

He tilted his head and gave her an exasperated look. 'Let's take it one step at a time. If we're happy with each other, and you think you can accept Katie and me as one item, we'll move on and tackle external irritations, I promise. I won't turn a blind eye if you feel unhappy about anything or anybody! If it's a question of you being worried about fitting in, if you feel uncomfortable, or you feel the slightest antagonism from anyone in the village, we'll go somewhere else. Remember you already have Emma on your side. She'll champion you because she already told me how much she likes you.' He paused. 'In fact it'll be up to you if we stay here, or move somewhere else. We don't have to stay here. I never lived in this house with Susan. I wanted a clean break after she died, so I sold the cottage where we'd been living and moved here. I refurnished everything because after a while I needed to move on. There are a few bits and pieces of family furniture from the past, but I wouldn't protest if you wanted to throw those out either. The furniture isn't important; you are. I can't imagine life without you anymore, Sara.'

She looked up at him and found herself responding despite her misgivings. 'You've really thought about it, haven't you? You've thought through what it means for all of us.' She freed her hand and put a finger on his lips. He kissed it, and she had to concentrate even harder on what she wanted to say.

Her vow not to get involved shattered. 'Perhaps you're looking too far ahead. You don't even know if we'll suit and get on yet.'

He grinned. 'That sounds a lot more encouraging. It doesn't matter how long we've known each other. I know what I feel. Nobody ever knows if they'll make it. The right-now feeling is how we decide to act. There's no point in speculating about the future. At least it sounds like you're prepared to consider the notion of you and me.'

Sara studied his familiar face. Was it a mistake to fall head over heels in love with Alex when she'd just been thinking about starting afresh in a new job, a new place? But she *was* in love with Alex; she had to accept that. She wanted him to hold her, she wanted his kisses and his caresses, and she wanted a great deal more. It wasn't just the physical attraction; it was everything Alex stood for.

'Will you give me some time so that I can sort it all out properly in my mind?

We have to be sure that this isn't just some flight of fancy. Katie will need to accept me being around all the time too. She's a delightful, thoughtful little soul, and I'm more than halfway to loving her already — but it won't be easy for her, either, to let someone else into your settled life.'

Alex's eyes sparkled and he nodded. 'She can be a little devil sometimes too. Of course we'll give ourselves time! I wasn't planning to throw you over my shoulders and carry you up to my bedroom — tempting though the idea is. You'll get all the time you want, I promise. I'll be as patient as I can. I just pray you don't turn me down.'

'Oh Alex!' Sara's hand crept around his neck and she drew him close until she could kiss him. 'I don't want to turn you down. I don't know why I've fallen in love with you in just a few days, but I have.' He gave her a brilliant smile and she continued. 'We have to be honest with each other, and then it will either come together, or fall apart.'

He was someone who was more than he appeared to be: a great father; a caring person; a good employer; someone who was liked in the village; someone who was prepared to take a risk to help someone like Peter, who was practically a stranger to him. Sara decided with a smile that she could look for the rest of her life and never find someone better.

Alex leaned forward and gave her a lingering kiss. Her lips parted to accept him at the first touch, and noting her reaction he increased the pressure. She couldn't think of anything because all her emotions were going haywire. She grabbed at him for balance, but everything around her still spun out of control. Caution went up in smoke and she returned his kiss. Whatever else happened, there was one thing she was certain of: he was what she wanted for the rest of her life.

With a slightly triumphant expression, he said, 'Let's take this little by little, okay?' She nodded. 'You've already decided to change your job anyway, so how about finding something that's within travelling distance of this place, so that we can see each other on a regular basis? That would be a great start.'

She looked over his shoulder at the garden covered in a blanket of snow. Some weak afternoon sunshine was trying to break through the grey clouds up above. Thinking about his words, she said, 'I wonder how Katie will feel.'

'I don't think you need to worry about Katie's reaction. She likes you a lot already, and I'm positive she'll protest loudly when you say you're leaving. I'm already beginning to worry how to get you alone when she's dancing around you all the time. You won't mind that too much, I hope?'

'What — that you need to split yourself between me and Katie? We both love you, Alex. Knowing you, I'm sure you'll be prepared to chop yourself in half to keep us both happy.'

He laughed. Reaching out for her, his

expression steadied as he pulled her closer and ran his free hand through her hair. 'Only you could have persuaded me to replace those carvings in the church. It was a dodgy business, and I had terrible pangs of conscience standing there thinking about what I'd done. I have no intention of committing hara-kiri as well.' Gazing into her face, he sent her pulse skidding at an even faster pace. 'I can only be grateful that you came into our lives when you did. I'll do my best to make you happy. What do you say? I love you. Will you give me a chance? Do you love me enough to give *me* a chance?'

Sara gazed at him for a moment, and there was stillness between them. She then smiled and said, 'Of course!' Reaching up with her hands, she cupped his face and kissed him with a hunger and reckless abandon. With her emotions spinning, she was aware that his lips were challenging and rewarding at the same time. She felt she'd come home at last.

17

Sara had never felt so wonderful. The next morning, when she woke from some of the best dreams she'd ever had, she just lay there and relished the thought that Alex had told her he loved her. They'd agreed to wait before they even hinted to anyone about things, mainly because they wanted to let Katie have more time to absorb the situation. Sara could tell the little girl liked her already, but perhaps slap-bang in the middle of the Christmas celebrations wasn't the right moment to announce her daddy had a girlfriend. There was plenty of time to put her in the picture. Sara admitted that she'd never felt more excited — like a bottle of champagne about to pop. She'd never felt she was walking on cloud nine with Rod or anyone else she'd met, but that was how she felt with Alex. She just needed to think of him to find she couldn't stop herself smiling.

At last she managed to think of other things and hurried to shower and dress, so that she could help Emma with the day's preparations. Alex and Katie were coming, and Paul was too.

Downstairs in the kitchen, Sara thought that Emma's mind seemed elsewhere this morning, and that was unusual. Sara had seldom met someone who was more organized and targeted, day after day. Even if she was wrapped in her own thoughts, it didn't stop her getting things ready for the buffet. By now she already had an impressive choice. Emma explained that the remains of the turkey were inside a crusty pie with onions and some mushrooms. There was a pile of traditional sausage rolls, a potato salad, and another salad of pasta, tomatoes and peppers. A thick vegetable soup was waiting on the hob, and she was arranging some crispy chicken drum-sticks on a large serving plate, because

Katie loved them. There were stuffed mushrooms, a massive trifle, individual chocolate mousse in glasses, and a centrepiece of her own beautiful Christmas cake decorated with skaters on an ice rink.

'Gosh, you must've been up since the crack of dawn,' Sara said.

Emma laughed. 'Some of it was frozen, and I made the cake weeks ago. Have some coffee and something to eat. You can help me prepare the dining room if you like.' She glanced at Sara briefly. 'You look very bright this morning.'

Sara coloured and took a quick sip of her coffee. 'Do I? The spirit of Christmas, I expect.'

Emma nodded. 'I want to decorate the table and sideboard in red and white. My biggest white tablecloth is over there, ready and waiting with some red serviettes. I bought a dozen red plates at one of our jumble sales earlier in the year, and they'll go well with the rest of the white plates. I bought some artificial shiny snowflakes at the Christmas market in town, and I thought we could hang them from the lamp over the table and over the sideboard. I dyed a table runner red, and we'll put the buffet on that, on the sideboard. Everyone can help themselves to the food. Together with my best crystal candlesticks and red candles, it should look very festive.'

'You've thought of everything, Emma. It already sounds perfect.'

'Well, you can start on it. I'm going to make some more coffee for when the others get up. They can eat in the kitchen this morning. I told Alex and Paul to come early enough so that we have plenty of time for Katie to open her presents, before we start to think about lunch.'

Sara's heartbeat quickened as she thought about seeing Alex again soon, and she was also looking forward to watching Katie open her presents. They'd all bought her something. Probably everyone was transported back to their own childhood and how excited they'd been about presents and Christmas.

She went into the dining room. Roland and Veronica came in soon after, and she sent them off to the kitchen. She switched on the lights on the tree and began setting the table. The red and white theme was perfect. Emma gave her the set of her best glasses from the sideboard cupboard, and she polished each one vigorously before Sara to set it on the table. Emma came back a second time with a flower arrangement of poinsettias and Christmas roses for the centre of the table. Sara stood back and admired the result.

'It looks wonderful, Emma.'

'And cost next to nothing.'

'I'll run upstairs and fetch my presents to go under the tree.'

Emma nodded. 'Mine are ready and waiting in the kitchen, and I think Peter has a plastic bag with some too.' She scuttled off, and when Sara returned the others were standing in the dining room with a glass in their hands, their presents under the tree and admiring the table decorations.

'Come and join us, Sara. Veronica and I bought some champagne yesterday. We're all toasting each other and Christmas.'

Sara accepted the glass and lifted it. 'Thank you. I wondered what Christmas would be like this year, because I was going to have to celebrate it on my own. It's turned out to be one of the best ever.'

Roland said, 'Yes, somehow Christmas is a magic blanket that wraps itself around us all, isn't it? It's our memories of things past, perhaps people who have already gone, but you usually remember them with a lot of pleasure. I don't suppose any of us remember a really terrible Christmas, do we? Veronica and I have been in places where soldiers spent their Christmas in a hospital bed, but even then the holiday cast a very special spell.'

Peter sounded philosophical when he

added, 'Yes, I think it's always a day of remembrance for adults, and one of joy for most children. Unfortunately not all over the world, but generally in the world we belong to. It's a day where we think of everything we've ever loved.'

Emma looked startled when she heard the doorbell. 'That's early for Alex and Paul. I hope nothing's happened to change their plans.' She hurried out, and they heard voices in the hall. Minutes later she returned with Ken at her side. 'Look who's come!' Her cheeks were bright red, and Sara was glad that Emma's flighty son had had enough sense to come after all.

'Hello, Ken!' She held out her hand. 'Merry Christmas.'

'Hello, beautiful! Merry Christmas! Mum forgot to hang some mistletoe in here, otherwise I'd be entitled to kiss you properly, but I suppose I'll have to do with a peck on your cheek.' He proceeded to do so, then moved on to shake hands with the others. Roland shoved a glass of champagne into his hands.

Ken lifted his glass and took a sip. 'I'm glad I came. This is good stuff.'

'Drink up,' Roland said. 'We bought enough for a party.'

'Speaking of parties, let's have some Christmas music, Mum, to put us all in the right mood.' He went over to the player and riffled through the CDs until he found one with Christmas jingles. Roland winced for a moment, but he soon got into the spirit and even waved his glass in time with the beat after a while.

Sara could tell how pleased Emma was to have Ken here today too. It was the icing on the cake for her. He was soon in his element, talking about his last visit to the south of France. Roland and Veronica had been posted to Marseille once for several weeks on a diplomatic mission, so they could chatter quite amiably about places they both knew. Peter had been to France several times, but Sara had only crossed the Channel once on a school outing. She didn't mind being a listener. She was pleased that Emma's Boxing Day celebrations were going with a bang.

Her insides fluttered like a captured butterfly in a cage when the doorbell announced the arrival of someone else. A minute or two later, Katie whirled into the room with her arms full of packages and beaming at everyone. Sara hoped her own uncontrollable love for Alex didn't show too blatantly on her face when he came in. He glanced briefly at the others, and then his eyes lingered on Sara and sent her a hidden message.

Trying to concentrate on other thoughts, she could see how impatient Katie was to get on with the present-giving. The little girl looked knowingly towards the presents in their coloured wrapping paper spread out beneath the tree. Just then, Paul's arrival completed the company, and he hurried to place his parcels before accepting a glass of champagne. To Sara's surprise, Ken exited and reappeared with a pile of presents too. Most of them looked like bottles, but she was glad he'd made an effort. She felt a stab of guilt when she realized she had nothing for him because she hadn't expected him to be here. Then she recalled that she'd bought the newest thriller the last time she went shopping.

Hurrying upstairs, she wrapped it up quickly in the remains of her Christmas paper. It wasn't the most attractive package when she finished, but it was better than nothing. Writing his name on it, she left her room in disarray and dashed back downstairs. The sound of laughter and chatter met her as she entered. She picked up her glass with her free hand and moved artfully near the tree. Finally she quickly put the parcel down with the others. Peter was bending too, placing something that looked like a paper bag with a bottle. She gave him a quick smile and wondered if he'd hurriedly found something for their unexpected visitor too.

Emma tapped her glass with a nearby knife to gain their attention. 'I think we're all in agreement that we exchange our presents before we have lunch.' She looked at Katie. 'I think some of us can hardly wait.' Katie looked up at her father, giggled and nodded vigorously.

Alex commented, 'After all the presents you got yesterday, I didn't think Father Christmas would bother to leave stuff for you here too. He must've got the addresses mixed up. It's clear that he's getting too old for all the work involved.' His grin flashed briefly.

Emma managed a tentative smile, but looked nervous when she said, 'Paul and I have something to tell you first.'

Paul moved across to stand by her side. 'I think everyone here knows what a treasure Emma is. I know that too, but not just because she's such a stalwart supporter of all the church activities. I've got to know her very well over the past couple of years, and gradually she's won a special place in my heart. I didn't dare to hope that she felt the same for me, but that's what's happened. We love each other, and we're planning to get married.'

There was a moment of utter silence as Sara stood opposite Ken. She could see the complete surprise on his face. Alex began to clap, and it was the signal for everyone else to join in. It gave Ken a moment to adjust. When the applause died down, Ken stepped forward and kissed his mother on her cheek.

She said, 'I'm so pleased you came and heard the news at the same time as everyone else has, love. I intended to phone you straight away, but this is much better.'

He smiled and shook Paul's hand before turning to face the others. 'I'm as surprised as the rest of you, but I wish Mum and Paul all the best. I already know that my mum is a treasure, and I hope Paul will always take care of her. I must admit it's astonishing to find that I'm going to have a new father at my age, but I know how long my mum's admired Paul and all the work he does in the village. She's bent my ear for ages telling me all about him. Maybe I should've expected it earlier, but I admit I didn't. I'd like you to lift your glasses and congratulate my mum and Paul, and wish them all the best for the future.'

'Congratulations, Paul and Emma!' echoed through the room.

Paul wrapped his arm around Emma's shoulder and beamed at her. Then, smiling at the gathering, he said, 'Thanks, Ken, and everyone else too. I know how much her son's approval means to Emma, and I promise you that I'll do my best to take care of your mother and make her happy.'

Ken ran his hand through his hair. 'Lord! This news will explode like a bomb in the village. Are you prepared to face the consequences?'

Paul laughed. 'I figure there'll be a lot of talk. But we'll cope — won't we, Emma?'

Katie didn't understand what all the fuss was about. She was getting impatient. 'Can we open the presents now?' she pleaded.

Emma nodded. 'Of course! You can read your own name on the parcels. Go on!'

Katie began to rifle through the packages while everyone else gathered around Emma and Paul to give them their own good wishes. The news had made a special day more special.

Sara met Alex's eyes as they stood waiting their turn. They seemed to tell her, *It'll be our turn next*. That didn't seem so unlikely anymore.

Sara kissed Emma on her cheek and shook Paul's hand. 'Great news! And how did you manage to keep it secret? In a place like this, that must've been quite a task.'

Paul laughed softly. 'Ah well, the fact that Emma's been busy helping me with parish affairs and supporting various groups and gatherings for years threw a smokescreen around us. I don't think she or I planned to ever marry again — did we, Emma?' She shook her head. 'But love grew, and that's what's going to happen. Somehow it seems as if it was meant to be.'

'I'm happy for you both. I don't think I can remember having a happier Christmas.'

Emma looked at her and then at Alex. He was helping Katie by holding the pile of parcels she'd found under the tree with her name on them. 'I wouldn't be surprised if the news about Paul and me sparks off some other good news soon. I hope so.'

Paul looked puzzled, and Sara coloured as she realized that Emma was a lot more perceptive than anyone suspected. She'd make a perfect vicar's wife.

Sara left them. She bent down to watch Katie opening her presents. The little girl's excited voice was louder than the sound of carols coming from the media centre. Katie threw her arms around Sara's neck, and Sara surrendered to her enthusiastic embrace. 'They're lovely, Sara! Just what I need for the hall. Thank you!'

Sara smiled. 'Are you sure they didn't come from Father Christmas?'

Trying to look grown up, and whispering, Katie said, 'I'm nearly six. I know all about Father Christmas. My friend Laura told me, and her brother told her. He's nearly nine, so he should know.'

Trying to look sensible, Sara said, 'You don't mind? About Father Christmas?'

'No. I did at first, but it doesn't really matter who gives the presents, does it? The main thing is we give and get presents, and love Christmas and the baby Jesus, isn't it?'

Sara could only admire how sensible she was. She couldn't remember how old she was herself when she'd found out there was no real Father Christmas, but she could remember that it upset her more than it had this little girl with her shiny curls and blue eyes.

'You'll come to see my doll's house tomorrow, won't you?'

Standing behind his daughter, Alex had a wicked grin on his face when he said, 'Yes, you must come. If you don't, Katie will be terribly disappointed — and I will too, of course!'

Other titles in the
Linford Romance Library:

WISHES CAN COME TRUE

Angela Britnell

Meg Harper is shocked when the man she knows as Lucca Raffaele, who stood her up in Italy the previous summer, arrives to stay at her family home in Tennessee — this time calling himself her step-cousin, Jago Merryn . . . Jago is there to acquire a local barbecue business, but discovering the woman who came close to winning his heart is only one of the surprises in store for him. Can they move past their mistrust and seize a second chance for their wishes to come true?

CHRISTMAS TREES AND MISTLETOE

Fay Cunningham

The idea of another family Christmas fills Fran with dread, particularly when she is asked to pick up her mother's latest charity case and bring him along. But Ryan Conway is not what she was expecting. He is looking after his young niece while his sister is in hospital, and Fran decides the pair of them may not be such bad company after all. Then, once the festivities are in full swing, Santa arrives unexpectedly — and Fran's life changes forever . . .

LOVE UNEXPECTED

Sarah Purdue

After being jilted by her fiancé, Nurse Jenny Hale decides to escape the well-meaning but suffocating sympathy of her friends and family by taking her honeymoon alone. On her journey to the Caribbean island of St. Emilie, a crisis throws her together with Doctor Luc Buchannan — who she finds herself falling for. But Luc also carries a heavy burden from his past. Is it possible for the doctor and the nurse to heal each other's hearts?

IT'S NEVER TOO LATE

Wendy Kremer

When Rebecca Summer is contracted to work as a temporary secretary for businessman Luca Barsetti on the Italian island of San Andrea, she thinks she can handle it — even though she was infatuated with him eight years ago at university. Much to her dismay, however, she finds that Luca's charms have not dimmed with time, and he appears to return her feelings. But she's now a confident, independent woman, far too sensible to fall head over heels for him again ... isn't she?